Praise for *Twelve*:

"*Twelve* . . . delivers a satirical, even playful portrait of a world that is perilous but essentially humane. . . . [McDonell] maintains a teasing affection for the absurdities of adolescence—an impressive feat of synthesis."                    —Jennifer Egan, *The New York Times Book Review*

"[McDonell] employs a prose style that affects pithiness and punch—a bit of Hemingway here, a bit of Hammett there, short paragraphs and terse dialogue—and that contains, beneath the tough-guy veneer, a soft inner core of sentimentality."

—Jonathan Yardley, *The Washington Post*

"The artfulness of *Twelve* is undeniable. The story moves, dips into big issues of race and class, and has great writing that reveals what McDonell calls 'the spiritual debilitation of a generation.'"

—Heidi Benson, *San Francisco Chronicle*

"An arresting debut . . . [McDonell] knows how to make you keep turning pages. . . . He knows how to establish a mood (completely creepy) that he sustains to the bitter, blood-soaked end."

—Malcolm Jones, *Newsweek*

"The novel, both an indictment of excess and a cry of teenage loneliness, is briskly paced and snappy, name-checking both Camus and Eminem in its sketches of the nihilistic spawn of Manhattan's big fish."

—Joe Heim, *People*

"Written with an exquisite eye for detail and character development . . . A worthy page turner."          —Deborah Schoeneman, *New York Post*

"There's no denying this young author's talent. . . . In cinematic style, McDonell cuts from one scene to another, one character to another. . . . Remarkable."          —Polly Paddock, *Charlotte Observer*

"A dramatic debut . . . An enthralling read about apathetic youth who have everything and nothing."          —Patty Lamberti, *Playboy*

# Twelve

## Nick McDonell

Grove Press
*New York*

*Published simultaneously in Canada*
*Printed in the United States of America*

Library of Congress Cataloging-in-Publication Data
McDonell, Nick.
Twelve : a novel / by Nick McDonell.
p. cm.
ISBN 0-8021-4012-2 (pbk.)
1. Juvenile delinquents—Fiction.
2. Manhattan (New York, N.Y.)—Fiction.   I. Title.
PS3613.C388 T84 2002
813'.6—dc21     2002020760


Grove Press
841 Broadway
New York, NY 10003


03 04 05 06 07   10 9 8 7 6 5 4 3

Dedicated to
my father

*Can we please all stand and have a moment of silence for those students who died. And can we now have a moment of silence for those students who killed them.*

# Part I
# Friday, December 27

# 1

WHITE MIKE IS thin and pale like smoke.

White Mike wears jeans and a hooded sweatshirt and a dark blue Brooks Brothers overcoat that hangs long on him. His blond hair, nearly white, is cropped tight around his head. White Mike is clean. White Mike has never smoked a cigarette in his life. Never had a drink, never sucked down a doobie. But White Mike has become a very good drug dealer, even though it started out as a one-shot deal with his cousin Charlie.

White Mike was a good student, but he's been out of school for six months, and though some people might wonder what he's doing, no one seems to care very much that he's taking a year off before college. Maybe more than a year. White Mike saw that movie *American Beauty* about a kid who is a drug dealer and buys expensive video equipment with the money he makes. The kid says that sometimes there is so much beauty in the world that sometimes you just can't take it. *Fuck that,* thinks White Mike.

White Mike is not looking at beauty. He is looking at the Upper East Side of Manhattan. It is two days after Christmas and all the kids are home from boarding school and everyone has money to blow. So White Mike is busy with a pickup in Harlem and then ounces and fifties and dimes and loud music and packed open houses and more rounds and kids from Hotchkiss and Andover and St. Paul's and Deerfield all looking to get high and tell stories about *how it is* to kids from Dalton and Collegiate and Chapin and Riverdale, who have stories, of their own. All the same stories, really.

The city is a mess this time of year, this year especially. Madison Avenue is all chewed up with construction, and there are more bums on Lexington than White Mike remembers. It is crowded on the sidewalks, and the more snow, the worse it gets, and there has been plenty of snow. On some streets when the snowdrifts pile up there is only a salted corridor of frozen dog shit and concrete. It's been cold since Thanksgiving, very cold, coldest winter in decades says the TV, but White Mike doesn't mind the cold.

*When White Mike first started dealing, it was summer and hot, and he tried to go as long as he could without sleep as a kind of experiment. White Mike already looked pale and scary to the kids he sold to, and then by the third day his jeans and white T-shirt were grimed out and he looked like some refugee James Dean, and the last hours were just a blur and the cars on the street flew past so close to him that people who saw flinched, but he had the cadences of the city down so tight that he was fine.*

*At Lexington and Eighty-sixth, his friend Hunter saw him and said, Mike, are you feeling okay, and White Mike turned to him and there was a smear of dirt on his face and his eyes were glowing in the neon light from the Papaya King juice/hot dog place. White Mike smiled at him and said watch this and took off running, just running so fucking fast up the block toward Park Avenue. There were a bunch of private school kids walking the same direction, and when they saw White Mike running past them, one of them said, loud enough for White Mike to hear, Madman running. And White Mike turned and walked back to them saying, Madman, madman, madman, madman, and the kids got scared, and then White Mike ran full into them, and they scattered, and they didn't think it was funny at all, and then White Mike started barking at them, howling, and they all ran. And White Mike ran after them, barking and howling, and Hunter ran after him, and White Mike let them get away after a couple blocks. Hunter put White Mike in a cab, but he had to convince the cabbie to take White Mike, and pay him in advance. The cabbie was jumpy and looked in the mirror at White Mike the whole ride. White Mike had his head out the window, staring at the pedestrians. When White Mike got home and collapsed in his bed with his shoes and clothes still on, his last thought before sleep was Why not? He had been awake for three days.*

White Mike gets out of a cab on Seventy-sixth Street and Park Avenue. He looks at the number of the cab: 1F17. He memorizes the number every time he gets out of a cab, in case he leaves anything behind. This has never happened.

Down Park Avenue there are Christmas lights wrapped around all the trees and bushes, and the wires give the snow better purchase, so the frost hangs low from the branches. When the lights turn on at night the trees almost disappear between the bulbs, and the disembodied points of light outline jagged constellations in the dark air. It is getting past dusk, and White Mike remembers one night, years ago, when his mother was still alive and she sat on the edge of his bed, tucking him in for the night, and told him about Chaos Theory. White Mike remembers exactly what she said. The story she told him was about how if a butterfly died over a field in Brazil and fell to the ground and made a mouse move or a tiny shoot of grass bend, then everything might be different here, thousands and thousands of miles away.

"How come?" he asked.

"Well, if one thing happens and changes something else, then that thing changes something else, right? And that change could come all the way around the world, right here to you in your bed." She tweaked his nose. "Did a butterfly do that?"

"Did the butterfly die?" he asked her back.

The lights on Park Avenue suddenly turn on. White Mike can feel his beeper vibrating again.

# 2

IT IS TEEN night twenty blocks uptown at the Rec. All the kids who show up to play basketball wear do-rags and Jordans, and they are all black. Two white kids show up, though, every once in a while. The wiry white kid is six feet tall and has the best ups of anybody but the worst ball-handling skills. His name is Hunter McCulloch, and he hustles all the time and makes some of his shots, so he gets to play. Hunter didn't know what was going on when he first came to the Rec. That was a couple years ago, when White Mike brought him. Everybody called each other *nigga*, and most of the conversation went by so fast that Hunter couldn't keep up. Ebonics, as White Mike said, existed. By now, though, Hunter is comfortable with it, and while he still doesn't use the word *nigga*, he knows what the *dill* is. Tonight the dill is this.

Nana is the best ball handler on the court. Fast, strong, and the color of coal under his white tank top, he is playing in a half-court game that Hunter watches from the sideline. Lanky Jerry, the only white kid in the place besides Hunter, is the big

man on the other team. Nana goes up for a shot, and Jerry
knocks him out of the air. Nana gets up and says something
fast about his neck hurting that Hunter can't understand, and
walks up off the court. He climbs up one of the spiral staircases
to the mezzanine and sits on the very top step, where he is
invisible to those below. His teammates yell that they know he's
up there *nigga* and to get his ass down and play. Nana ignores
everybody. So someone on Nana's team looks to the sidelines
and says he needs one. Hunter takes Nana's spot. It is toward
the end of the night, and no one else is waiting except a short
Puerto Rican kid named Arturo who just hangs around and
doesn't get to play much.

Hunter's doing fine, but the game stops again when Nana
comes down and demands his spot back. "I'm playin'."

"What?" says Hunter. From his first time at the Rec, he
never wanted to cause any trouble and sometimes even apologized to his teammates when he fouled or missed a shot. No
one else ever apologized, but Hunter was a likable white kid
who could get boards, so nobody really thought any less of him.

"I said gimme my fuckin' spot back."

"Okay." Hunter shrugs and moves to get off the court. All
the other kids look at one another. This is not cool.

"Yo, man, don't let him do that," says the kid who asked
Hunter to fill Nana's spot. "He left. It's your game."

"Nah, it's okay."

"No, you don't have to get off the court, man, he left. You
were playin'. Stay."

"What did you say?" says Nana.

"I said he should stay. You left. You got next."

"No, I got next," says Arturo.

"Shut up, Arturo," everyone says.

Hunter is thinking that everyone learns compromise. Maybe in history class, where Hunter learned about Henry Clay, the Great Compromiser. But Clay never played here at the Rec.

"Nana, get off the court. Hunter's my nigga," another black kid says to Nana, and gives Hunter the pound. Everyone laughs except Nana. Nana is pissed and gets up in Hunter's face. Hunter has no idea what to do. He backs off. The rest watch. Arturo perks up and starts yelling *fight*, gets all interested. Nana is talking mad smack.

Hunter is a pretty beef kid. It is a kind of flowing beefness. Not thick like a bull. Just this stack of muscle and sinew. So when Hunter finally hits Nana, Nana gets rocked. Slow it down, the way they do in instant replays, and you can see his jaw move laterally with the blow. Frame by frame it is deeply gruesome, worse than anything most of the kids have ever seen. Everyone grimaces at the solid smack of fist on flesh.

Of course Hunter hasn't hit first, he's just reacted. He ran around the gym away from Nana a bunch of times before he was cornered and turned and unloaded. He immediately says, "Man are you okay, I didn't mean to hurt you, you just got to cool it," and "God damn" as Nana swings again and he ducks. Nana shoots him an elbow to the ear, and Hunter stumbles. Hunter suddenly understands that Nana is for real. Nana charges and gets a knee to his teeth. Blood smears all over the two of them as they thud to the ground.

No one knows what to do. This is a real fight and no one fights at the Rec, although everyone says there was a stabbing last summer. Finally, the other kids pull Hunter and Nana apart after they have been rolling around on the floor for a while. Hunter is pissed and bleeding now too, and Nana is yelling, and the gym is as loud as it has ever been. Arturo thinks this is the coolest thing he has ever seen and walks up to tell Hunter to go and kick the nigger's ass some more. Hunter tells him to get the fuck away. Nana yells to see if Arturo wants some. Arturo doesn't, but he calls Hunter a pussy and turns to walk. Hunter is crazed. This is too much. He grabs a basketball and hurls it at the back of Arturo's head, hitting him dead on. Arturo falls down face first. Nana says fuck this shit and goes to get his stuff. Arturo throws the ball back but won't really fuck with Hunter. He saw what happened.

Nana doesn't look at Hunter anymore, just walks out covered with blood. Hunter watches him go. There is blood all over him too. He's not really even sure what happened.

# 3

WHITE MIKE WALKS into the gym and brushes past a strong dark kid he knows from uptown, hurrying down the stairs. White Mike watches after him and wonders where all the blood came from. Inside, he sees Hunter at the far end of the gym shooting free throws by himself. He has not seen Hunter since September, but the two go way back. They went all through grammar school together, wearing blue blazers and ties every day. Once they went on a field trip to Central Park with their class, and people kept yelling out "Dead Poets Society" as they passed by. White Mike liked the trip. It was like some experimental class; they sat on a bench somewhere and looked hard at everything for a couple of minutes. No talk, just watching. Tried to cool off a little, tried to see things a little more clearly. And White Mike looked at his classmates and thought, *Recognize this: we're only grammar school kids dressed like investment bankers.* Hunter had understood. White Mike sees the blood on Hunter from halfway across the gym.

"Hunter."

"Hey, Mike, can you believe this shit?" Hunter says, turning and tossing White Mike the ball. "One-on-one?"

White Mike catches it. "I don't play anymore."

"You're kidding."

"Did you fight that kid?" White Mike throws the ball back.

"Nana. He's crazed."

"How's school?"

"Same. Still dealing?"

White Mike shrugs.

"Rich yet?"

"I'll buy you dinner."

As they walk out, Hunter says to White Mike, "I read somewhere that even if you're really broke, you'll survive, because there is so much food in New York just thrown away on the streets that it's nearly impossible to starve."

"You have to want to eat."

There is a McDonald's almost next door to the Rec. Hunter and White Mike sit by the window. Outside it is starting to snow again. The snow is wet and heavy, and it sticks to the plastic window and slides down, blurring the lights of the cars moving downtown. Hunter asks White Mike about college, if he's thinking about going.

"Maybe."

"What does that mean?"

"It means maybe."

"You've got till January first, man. You're fucked if you haven't applied yet."

"I deferred last year. I've got until May to tell them."

"My dad told me if I didn't get into Harvard, I had to go to Dartmouth."

"He went there, right?"

"My grandfather gave them a science building."

"Well, go to Harvard and you'd get to be with Warren." Warren is their other best friend from high school. He is White Mike's year.

"See, exactly," says Hunter.

"Exactly what?"

"Warren got into Harvard. You think you couldn't rip that place up? Come on, it could be the three of us together. Old times." Hunter is laughing. "You'd be my year."

"Yeah, just what I want. Old times." White Mike feels his beeper going off in his pocket, probably that kid throwing the party in that town house off Fifth in the Nineties. "Got to go."

# 4

BY THE MIDDLE *of the fall, White Mike was dealing seriously, waiting for a customer on East End Avenue one day when he saw a kid throw a lit cigarette off a fire escape, and he watched it land in an open garbage can full of dry cardboard and newspaper. A fire started in the can, slowly at first, sending little whorls of thin smoke into the air but picking up force until the edges of the newspapers curled in the heat and the air in the cardboard popped. And then, as the flames started to lick at the metal, a mass of fire shot up and the tin can turned red around the rim, and the kids on the fire escape came down to the street. There, they pretended to be homeless around the garbage-can fire.*

*White Mike watched this and thought about* The Plague, *about how this town gets shut down by a plague and in the beginning all the rats start dying, before the disease hits the people. The rats come out into the street to die. They just die by the truckload, and the people have to make big piles of rats and incinerate them.*

# 5

HUNTER PUTS ON his headphones as he watches White Mike get into a cab. He wants to walk. He is thinking about Nana, and then he isn't thinking about anything. The city, in case you don't know, is better at night. It is cooler and gives you a second wind and is clearer, but it is snowing harder now and getting colder. Hunter keeps walking anyway. He is listening to James Taylor. At Park and Seventy-ninth, his CD is on the last track. He wants it to end as he walks through the door of his family's co-op, so he restarts to "Fire and Rain" and sets it on repeat. Hunter doesn't ever let anyone know that he listens to James Taylor, but the lie doesn't bother him because he suspects that everybody listens to softer music and hides it.

*Sweet dreams and flying machines in pieces on the ground,* as he walks past his doormen who nod at him. He hits the elevator button, leans against the wall. The doors open and he steps in, leans again, and stares at the ceiling. There is a hole in the middle of the glass light fixture, which Hunter knows conceals a camera. He didn't realize this until after he had taken

out his eleven-year-old prepubescent wanker and jiggled it about
in the elevator, flapped it between his legs, humping air before
he knew about humping. He didn't know why he did it while
he was doing it, and he still doesn't know why he did it. The
super showed him the tape when he turned fifteen. *I've seen
fire. . . .*

Hunter realizes the song is still going to be playing after
he steps through the door of his apartment, but so what.

He's inside his apartment now and hears the television in
the library—some show he can't name. He walks in, and his
father is sitting there drinking, being sad. Hunter's father is a
big man, bigger than his son, always drinking, always sad. His
mother too. At least that's the way it seems to Hunter.

"Hunter, come talk to me."

Hunter wonders what's on his father's mind this time. He's
leaving for Europe tomorrow. His mother is already there. They
ought to be happy. Isn't that the way it's supposed to be. Hunter
listens to his father talk about how hard he studied when he was
at boarding school, and then how hard he worked at Dartmouth,
and how hard he still has to work. He looks like he might cry.
After as much as he can take, Hunter says he's tired and wants
to go to bed, and he goes down the hall to his room. His father
didn't even notice the blood.

Hunter lies down on his bed with his clothes on. He knows
he won't be able to sleep and just waits it out until he hears his
father go to bed, then gets up and slips out. He wants to walk.
*And I've seen rain . . . James Taylor sucks,* thinks Hunter.

# 6

NANA LIVES ON 117th Street and Third Avenue. There is this hill that descends from Ninety-sixth Street on the east side and ends in Harlem. One minute Park Avenue is doormen and Audis, and the next it is Harlem. One of the first things you see as you pass Ninety-sixth Street on Third Avenue is a bad fried-chicken joint. Nana hates the place. For him, it is always a lot better going down to the Rec than it is coming back uptown, coming home.

Home is his mother's apartment on the eighth floor of the project, 2123 Third Avenue, past the big sign that says WELCOME TO JEFFERSON HOUSES. Nana walks along the curved path to the entrance and around the corner of the front building, the one that hides the monkey bars from the street. His building's door faces the playground. Nana turns the corner thinking about how he's gonna have to explain all the blood on his clothing to his mother.

On the far side of the doorway, he sees two men. He can't really make them out as he walks toward the door. They're both tall, one slim and one heavy, both puffy in their huge North Face parkas. And the slim one is white. *Strange,* Nana thinks. Must be some kind of deal happening. Nana steps back around the corner where they can't see him and peers around.

"You fuckin' guy, you're doing it, aren't you," says the heavy one. Pissed, but calm pissed. *Scary pissed,* thinks Nana. "I told you not to do any of this shit."

"No, man." The white guy is edgy, muttering.

"Fine. Gimme the money."

"Okay, let me get it." The white guy reaches into his pocket and Nana can see him go all tense, and the big man sees it too, because as the white guy is bringing up a gun, a small silver thing with a flash of pearl handle, the big man punches him. The white guy staggers back.

Then, in a fluid movement the heavy man reaches in his pocket and suddenly there is a gun with a hand towel wrapped around it pointing at the white kid. The big man pulls the trigger, and Nana flinches as the muffled explosion blasts and echoes around the block. The towel catches fire, and the big man throws it on the ground as the white guy is sliding down the wall, leaving a track of blood and down feathers from his parka.

Nana bolts for the stairs, thinking the shooter is taking off the other way, but the heavy man changes his mind and turns around. Nana looks him straight in his brown and yellow bloodshot eyes for a split second before he gets kneed in the testicles and falls to the ground. He squirms in anguish and, out of the corner of his eye, sees the heavy man back up. Nana tries to crawl up and away. He gets a good look at the corpse. The guy isn't much more than a kid. Pale with blond, almost white hair, and eyes frozen open. As Nana tries to rise, the heavy guy's boot misses his temple and hits him in the side of the mouth. He goes back down and doesn't see any more as the heavy man scrambles for the towel, wraps it around the gun, and shoots him in the head. The heavy man turns back to the white corpse and picks up the little silver gun.

# 7

IT'S BEEN A great vacation so far. Lots of parties. Sara Ludlow and one of her girlfriends are walking to another one. They step carefully to avoid wetting their Jimmy Choo knee-high stiletto boots in the puddles of slush. Sara is rooting through the Prada bag she got for Christmas, looking for her compact. She wants to see how she looks. Everyone pays attention to how Sara looks.

Sara Ludlow is the hottest girl at her school by, like, a lot. When that kid Chris, whose house she is going to, made up the chart about where the girls stood, like the stock-market quotes, Sara always came up on top. Her line on the chart kept rising while other girls tumbled according to the whims of the market or whether they put out. When the chart was finally discovered taped behind the Bob Marley poster in the senior lounge, the girls were fascinated. Egos were crushed and inflated, but no one was really surprised by Sara's dominance. Long legs, large breasts, blond hair, blue eyes, high cheekbones. Even people who didn't like her said that she was great-looking—if you were looking for that conventional sort of beauty. Such statements rarely assuaged any jealousy.

Sara looks in her mirror as she talks to her girlfriend. "Who's gonna be there?"

"Mostly seniors, I hope. It's that kid Chris's house, and his brother is supposed to be back from boarding school or rehab or whatever he goes to now."

"Claude?"

"Yeah. Supposedly he's clean now."

"Whatever. Did you notice Jessica got a nose job?"

"Really? I couldn't tell." *Ha, ha, ha.*

"Yeah, me either. You know who's a bitch?"

"Who?"

"Layla."

"Yeah, I know. She thinks she is so smart. She never shuts up."

"She's in my English class."

"Wenchler's?"

"Yeah, and she just says anything. Something about how everyone took the holocaust so seriously or something. She made Jane Grey run out of the room crying."

"Jane cries all the time."

"I know, but Layla was, like, heartless."

"Is Jane Jewish?"

"No, I don't think so. She used to be anorexic."

The girls are having a big laugh over that one when they get to Ninetieth Street and Madison. They can see the town house where the party is happening. There is a tall kid in an overcoat standing in the doorway.

# 8

WHITE MIKE CAN hear some pop rap playing inside. Nelly or something:

> *Oh why do I live this life*
> *Hey, must be the money.*

This is Chris's house and Chris's party. Chris hands White Mike a hundred dollars and asks if he wants to come in. White Mike doesn't. He glances over his shoulder at the two girls coming up the steps. He stares at the pretty one for a second, wonders how smart she is, then leaves.

White Mike walks west, crosses Fifth Avenue, and turns downtown along the east side of the park. The apartment buildings across the street are like fortresses. White Mike thinks about how rich everyone is. *So you are born in the capital of the world and you can never escape and that's how it is because that's how everyone wants it to be. It is all about want. No one needs anything here. It is about when you wake up in the morning and the snow is already coming down and it is bright between the build-ings where the sun falls but already dark where the shadows are, and it is all about want. What do you want? Because if you don't want something, you've got nothing. You are adrift, you are washed away, and then buried under the snow and the shadows. And when, in the spring, the snow melts, no one will remember where you were frozen and buried, and you will no longer be anywhere.*

# 9

CHRIS WAITS AT the door for the two girls. *Sara Ludlow,* Chris thinks, *Sara Ludlow. I wonder if she's still going out with that football-player guy.* That would be just his luck. Part of the bad luck of not ever getting laid, even though Chris is seventeen and a half years old and has dark blond hair and blue eyes and is good enough looking, except for the acne, which is part of the bad luck, the same bad luck that he has felt come back to him over and over since he was little. Bad luck like a couple of months ago when he was trying to hook up with some public school girl, and she was so turned on or surprised or whatever when he put his fingers between her belt and her belly to try to ease her pants down that she jerked around suddenly, and Chris's left pinky got snapped back, and the tendon in that finger tore in two, and the bottom half retracted down into his palm. He had no control over the digit; it hung limp as he moved the rest of his fingers. The girl thought it was funny. He told everyone he had gotten his hand stuck in a drawer, but he wound up with a big cast from the complicated hand surgery and lost his confidence. So he waited. And now that the cast is gone and he is mobile and, to his mind, attractive again, he throws parties, looking for the right girl. And here suddenly is Sara Ludlow asking him to show her around.

"I hope it's a big party," Sara says. "They're more fun." Chris doesn't know what to say to that, but he is feeling lucky.

The stone town house rises, clutched in ivy, up from the sidewalk. If you were to take the stairs on a normal weekday, you would be in the perfect artisan sterility of the extremely wealthy. Nothing out of place; tapestries on the walls, real ones, from dead monks near Normandy. Tonight, though, there is a party going on. The tapestries are still there, but things (bodies, cans, parkas, portable DVD players) lie out of place.

On the sixth floor, a bunch of kids are standing around another kid who is banging on a drum set in an empty guest bedroom. One of them is playing the drums, but his rhythm is suffering for the eight beers he's had. Lots of beers—Corona Lights, Budweisers, all over the floor in various parts of the house. Across the hall from the drum room a stereo is playing Ben Harper's "Burn One Down" loud enough so the kids smoking weed on the terrace can hear it. They look out over the street and flick ashes into the ivy. On the fifth floor, there are only two kids, one blond and one dark and pimply, both short and passed out on big leather couches where some other kids left them entwined and drooling. On the fourth floor, about ten kids sit in front of a big flat-screen TV watching Cinemax pornography. One kid, in a big leather chair, has a girl half sitting on his lap. They both stare at the screen happily, the boy's left hand resting lightly on the left half of the girl's left breast. On the third floor, more kids are sitting around a table, drinking and gossiping and flirting. Snoop plays on that stereo.

"You should have invited more people," Sara Ludlow says to Chris. All he can think about is what it would be like to fuck Sara Ludlow and not just hook up with some drunk girl at one of his parties, like is happening in a different room on the third floor where a girl they both know named Jessica is making out with a guy from another school whose name nobody knows. Jessica and this guy, and they are reduced to really just the two of them, making out without any pretense or thought about it. And then he comes in his pants and they stop and the guy goes to get another beer and Jessica goes to the bathroom.

# 10

JESSICA STARES INTO the mirror. She doesn't wear much makeup. She is not flawless, like Sara Ludlow, but she is pretty. The nose job helped. Creamy skin, long brown hair, big brown eyes. A guy once thought he was mad funny when, teasing one of her admirers, he cupped his hands in front of his nipples and said Jessica had big brown eyes. And she does have nice breasts. And thin lips, a cruel mouth sort of, but nobody would ever say "cruel mouth." Tonight she wears dark pants, slung just below her hips to reveal the band of her panties that say Calvin Klein. Her ribbed sweater shows off her body but no skin, except when she stretches and you can see her navel as her sweater lifts. She is not fat, but she is not skinny. She is healthy-looking. She is a jock: soccer, swimming.

This was Jessica on the phone a few hours ago with one of her admirers, another guy who has heard she is wild:

"I'm really comfortable with my body," she says.

"Meaning you're hot?"

"Like, thighs are a big deal, you can't have big thighs, but me . . ."

"So what kind of thighs do you have?"

"Strong thighs. Swimming makes them that way."

In the spring Jessica runs track and good for her, but tonight, right now, she has not gone into the bathroom to relieve herself. She has gone into the bathroom to do some coke before that drunk boy comes back. Everyone else smokes weed and drinks. They think it's crazy to do coke except on special occasions, like proms. Not Jessica. So out comes the little Baggie filled with white powder. A chemist would have found the contents of this bag interesting. It is not cocaine. It is something else—*number twelve,* the boy called it when he handed it to her and said to save it for them for later—and as soon as Jessica takes her first hit, everything changes.

Her fine eyebrows arch up above her eyes and her mouth opens. She sits down heavily on the toilet and leans back. She feels that tingling. Chills down the spine. Maybe like when you first read that part of the Gettysburg Address. Maybe. Yes, Jessica is a very good student, yes, early decision from Wesleyan next year. The Gettysburg Address. She read all about Lincoln in her advanced-placement American history class. Read about Lincoln and even felt that shot up her spine when she read those words to herself, late one night, memorizing the speech for homework. She liked it better than anybody. The Gettysburg Address: *that from these honored dead we take increased devotion to that cause for which they gave the last full measure of devotion; that we here highly resolve that these dead shall not have died in vain . . .*

But not really. Jessica does another hit, and the tingling gets fuller and goes from her spine into the back of her head.

*. . . But, in a larger sense . . .*

She locks her knees and tightens her buttocks and rests the back of her head on the top of the tank.

*. . . we cannot dedicate . . .*

A huge grin breaks out over her face, and the colors of the bathroom dance in her vision.

*. . . we cannot consecrate . . .*

Jessica giggles and flows off of the toilet, her face sliding easily against the porcelain and leaving a trail of sweat.

*. . . we cannot hallow—this ground.*

*White Mike stood up and buttoned his blazer and walked to the head of the class. He said in a clear voice that his report was about Abraham Lincoln because he was so tall. The class laughed, even the teacher, because he knew White Mike was joking and it would be an excellent report. White Mike started reading. Abraham Lincoln became a martyr, he said, the same way that JFK would become one. In his conclusion, White Mike said that death does not vindicate. It might have been good for the country, but it wasn't good for Abraham, and it wasn't good for Jack. And it wasn't good for me, thought White Mike, whose mother had died the day before. White Mike's father said he didn't have to go to school, and White Mike said, What will that do?*

# 11

SARA LUDLOW HAS been at Chris's party for an hour now, and she is not impressed. She doesn't want a joint or a beer, and she is especially bored by the story Chris tells her about how his brother got his first blow job at a bat mitzvah. She says it's time for her to leave.

"Where's your boyfriend?" Chris asks.

Sara looks at him for a moment. He might be useful. "Driving in from East Hampton," she says. "Where's your brother?"

# 12

CHRIS'S BROTHER, CLAUDE, walks down Mulberry Street in his dark green North Face parka. In his pockets he is carrying: one clear plastic prism filled with weed, one Coach wallet containing $965, one fake ID (repeating hologram of the Ohio state flag, the buckeye, his picture, and a fake name, laminated, purchased from a card shop on Bleecker Street; the guy who sold it said, "Never fails, forty dollars"), one school ID, one Citibank ATM card, one American Express Platinum card, one naked picture of drunk ex-girlfriend whom he fingered while they watched the Blue Man Group with a bunch of other kids, two MetroCards, and one Nokia cell phone that says "Pussy monger!" when it turns on.

Claude is six feet two inches tall. He walks with his hood up, hands thrust in his pockets, face hidden. He is much more handsome and strong than his brother; the same fair coloring that doesn't burn in the sun, but perfect skin and an angular face. He is taking a fifth year of high school at a bad boarding school, and even there he is not a good student or a good athlete, though he lifts a lot. He listens to rap and metal. He used to do blizzards of cocaine. There is a famous story about him that all the kids know. The story goes that one night, in a bar, he walked up to some kids with his huge pet snake coiled around his neck and shoulders. He didn't know the kids, but they went to some private school, so he knew what they were. And he pushed up against the biggest kid, rubbing the snake on his shoulder. The kid was scared silent—he just stood there, trying to wait it out, whatever it was. Claude didn't want to wait, of course, so he started pushing the snake up toward the kid's face. The kid backed away, and somebody yelled for Claude to back off, which gave the kid more balls, and so he said, *Yeah, man, what's the idea?*, then laughed a nervous laugh. He knew he had to make it all funny. And Claude was smiling too. Then, out of nowhere, or so it seemed to everyone there, Claude hooked the inside of the kid's cheek with his forefinger and yanked back violently. The cheek ripped with an audible tear, and all this blood fell on the bar and into the martinis. The kid was screaming and clutching his face, and Claude just walked out of the bar. Everybody knows this story.

Claude's friend Tobias was with him that night and is with him again now. He is walking down the street next to Claude, dressed the same way. His hood is back, though. And where Claude is handsome, Tobias is beautiful. Not quite effeminate, just beautiful. Tobias is a part-time model. There is a famous story about him too. It's about how when Tobias was twelve, he took a shit in his bed just so the maid would have to clean it up. Tobias bragged about it the next day at school, and nobody laughed harder than Claude. Tobias is still proud of the story and tells it a lot, and when he does, there is still nobody who laughs harder than Claude.

So now the two of them are walking down Canal Street in Chinatown. *Slantyville* is what they call it. It's a trip down there, for them for sure. First they smoked, of course. And they have already bought a skinned rabbit from one of the windows where it was hanging. They carried the rabbit around for a while, then threw it in the open back window of a passing yellow cab. Now they stop by a trinket shop. There are weapons in the window. Sais and nunchakus and great replica samurai swords. Claude and Tobias are not samurais, but they like swords and are still a little fucked up. They walk in.

It is much brighter inside than Claude expects. There is a TV going with a tape of a karate sparring match playing. Beneath the glass counter there are knives for sale. One is especially long and bright, a butterfly knife with blades that slide in and out of the shaft. Claude taps the glass over the knife and indicates to the middle-aged Asian woman behind the counter that he wants it. She takes it out and hands it to him. Claude runs his soft hands up and down the blade. The woman is tiny and fat, and she nods and smiles in anticipation of the sale and takes the blade back from Claude.

"Look," she says. She spins her wrist, and there is a metallic swish as the blades open out. Light bounces off the blades onto the walls and reflects off the glass over the framed *Enter the Dragon* poster. Claude is transfixed.

The lady puts the knife on the counter, satisfied with her demonstration. "Here," she says, and reaches for a different weapon. A bola, small and painful, with brass orbs to shatter shins and skulls. She holds the rope and clacks the brass together, and the sound is loud and sharp. Claude watches the orbs go and almost grabs them out of her hand. He tests their weight as if to throw them. He holds one of the brass spheres to his cheek and feels the chill metal against his pores. He puts the bola down next to the knife and points to the halberd in the window.

"Ah," sighs the lady. Of course. She pads to a back room where there are two more such spears leaning in a corner, behind a box of miniature Statues of Liberty and New York snow globes. She brings one back to the counter and places it before Claude.

"No case?" he asks.

"Sorry," she says, and wraps a cloth around the crescent ax head and the point of the spear. Claude pays her, and she smiles and nods. Claude puts the spear and bola in his bag, and the knife in its plastic case in his inside coat pocket, where he can feel it against his chest. The shaft of the spear sticks out of his bag and bangs the door frame as he walks out. Then Claude turns back to the woman and slurs out, "Hoh, tenk veddy much, my little yellow-skinned sister." Tobias can't stop laughing.

Claude and Tobias stop at several similar shops before they find the subway and head back uptown. At the end of the night, nunchakus and throwing stars, sharp and bright, and a double-bladed sword and brass knuckles and two sais and a knife disguised as a fountain pen are all on Claude's person or in his bag and clinking. Tobias thinks the night is a riot, and laughs some more and tells Claude he's one crazy fucker before they part ways at the subway stop at Eighty-sixth and Lexington.

When Claude gets home, his brother's party is still going on but he doesn't care. He is a samurai, his bag heavy with weapons. In his room, he takes all the clothing out of a wardrobe and shoves it under his bed. He opens his bag and arranges the knives and swords with care. In less than an hour, Claude steps back from the closet and admires his careful work. Closed, the wardrobe looks like a regular closet, an oaken antique. Open it and the weapons glint in the half-light, arranged in some perfect order like a private shrine.

# 13

SAMURAI HAVE BEEN White Mike's favorites since he saw them in cartoons when he was eight. When he was twelve, he read *Shogun* over Easter break and thought about dying with honor. What he imagined to be samurai music would play in his ears. Walking the street, White Mike would run and jump off railings, bringing an imaginary samurai sword down upon imaginary foes, maintaining the all-important *chundan*, middle ground. A year or two later he would equate all this with *amor fati* when he finally got around to reading Nietzsche—the idea that you must love whatever comes, joy or sorrow, pain or happiness. After he read Nietzsche, everything made a lot more sense.

So White Mike lives in his apartment, which is big and empty, with his father whom he never sees, and looks out the window at the night, and forces himself to be content. He forces himself to enjoy reading, or watching television, or preparing a meal, or doing his laundry, or spending the money he has made, or whittling a tiny bird, like he is doing now at the kitchen table with an expensive handmade pocketknife he purchased. It is a forcing.

Or later, up in his room, at his desk, White Mike has the lights on and spreads all the weed out on his desk, and it sits before him in different piles, different amounts, and it is nothing new. And he is compelled to order it and organize it and store it away for sale later because it is the most important thing he does. It is what he does, and so it will be done precisely, and with nothing else in mind. Because what else is there to do?

## GRADE 11

*English:* 97
*Mike has been an active participant in the discussions of* King Lear *and is always thoughtful and inquisitive in class. He wrote a remarkably original and thoroughly documented term paper on the difficult topic of "Nietzschean Existentialism," as he called it; though, as with the rest of his work, it did not seem to be very satisfying to him.*

*Latin:* 98
*A truly dedicated student. Mike's translations continue to be written with a passion and interest uncommon in students his age. He could be more forgiving to his classmates, however. He is, at times, extremely impatient.*

*Mathematics:* 98
*Although Mike is a fine student, he is clearly uninterested in mathematics.*

*Science: 69*
*Mike is clearly a bright young man, but he simply does not do the work. While all of his test scores are in the 90s, without comple-tion of the lab reports it is impossible for me to give him a grade above merely pass.*

*History: 96*
*Mike wrote a superb term paper, beautifully researched and highly informative. What he needs to learn is the give-and-take of discussion.*

*Homeroom Comments:*
*Mike excels in what pleases him and does dismally in what does not. All of us at the school sympathize with the recent tragic event, but it is also our responsibility to point out that his continued disciplinary problems only undermine his future. Although I find Mike charming and have come to think of him as a friend as well as a student, his manner can be off-putting. At times he can seem quite distant, although I do not believe he is ever bored. Mike has many gifts. He may even have genius in him, although many of us who have taught him agree that it is very frustrating trying to bring it out. He is old enough now for it to be up to him.*

# 14

IT IS VERY late when Chris goes to the bathroom and finds Jessica passed out on the floor by the toilet. He looks at her for a long time. Jessica is his friend, but he never gets to stare at a live girl like this. He likes it.

# 15

IN WHITE MIKE's tenth-grade year, there was a rapist at large: the Upper East Side Rapist. Some girl named Megan in his ethics class told White Mike that, "But no, seriously, being raped is like my greatest fear. I'm, like, so seriously afraid of being raped. Just two days ago, the rapist walked into a store in the middle of the day, locked the door, and raped a clerk. Will you walk me home?"

White Mike just shrugged and started walking with her toward her house at Ninety-eighth and Fifth Avenue. He told her that she had nothing to worry about if she was alert. When they were just getting to Engineer's Gate leading up to the Reservoir, they stopped and looked at the runners.

"It's not scary here," White Mike told her, "there is probably no place in the world where you're safer."

On his way back downtown, White Mike stopped in a deli for chocolate milk, and there was a flyer with a sketch of the suspected rapist on the wall. White Mike thought it looked like every other sketch of a criminal he had ever seen. A nondescript young black man in a hooded sweatshirt, like the one he wore *under his overcoat. He pictured that man holding down Megan (who was, like, so afraid and screaming) and ripping her plaid-skirt school uniform and probably just raping her right there in the middle of Fifth Avenue. He suddenly felt real bad for both of them.*

# Part II
# Saturday, December 28

# 16

*A BLACK KID and a white kid with fake IDs from Ohio and Oregon, fucked-up dead on 117th Street.*

*God I hate drugs,* thinks one of the detectives investigating the double murder at the Jefferson Houses housing project. He is now at the Rec. He spoke with Nana's mother, and she told him that's the last place her son was. Of the kids there the night before, only Arturo is around. So when the detective asks if anyone knows this kid Nana, they all say yes, but only Arturo says he saw him last night.

"Were you his friend?"

"Yeah, we were tight."

"Was he ever in any kind of trouble?"

"No, that kid was great, man, straight."

"How was he last night?"

"I'll tell you, this punk kid, Hunter, just started fuckin' with him. I think he was racist or something like that, Detective. One of them Nazis."

"What happened?"

"Well, they fought, you know, and I broke 'em up, but Hunter was pissed that I stopped it and took off. But you know I was just looking out for my boy."

The other players on the sideline roll their eyes as they overhear. The detective doesn't notice.

"You think this kid Hunter might have messed with Nana some more?"

"Yeah, man, you never know with guys like that. He was crazy."

The detective thanks Arturo and heads downstairs. He looks up Hunter's mailing address in the Rec's files.

As the detective arrives in the McCulloughs' lobby, so too does Hunter, finally tired from hours of wandering the streets. After he went out at three, he walked all the way down to the Village and sat through part of a movie on Fourteenth Street. After it was over he strolled up Sixth Avenue and across the park. He has a bag of doughnuts he bought somewhere. The detective sees the dried blood and asks him if he is Hunter. Hunter says yes, and the detective says he's bringing him in for questioning. The doormen don't know what to do. The detective can't believe this, it's too easy, but the kid is covered with blood.

In the police car, Hunter thinks about how his father is on a plane to Europe and his mother is already there, and how he doesn't have any phone numbers for them. If it weren't Saturday, he could call his father's office to get them to track him down. As soon as he was off the plane. He could call White Mike, but White Mike is a drug dealer and what kind of idea is that. He thinks about the other numbers he knows by heart.

Not many, and none seem to fit. But he does have this kid Andrew's phone number with him. Andrew went to a different school, and they knew each other only because their fathers work together, but they had hit it off. Hunter figures that maybe Andrew's father will be able to help.

By the time Hunter gets to make this call, a sample of the blood on his shirt is on its way to the lab.

## 17

WHEN THEY WERE all little kids, Hunter and White Mike and Warren and White Mike's cousin Charlie went to the Central Park Zoo. Warren's nanny, an excellent tiny woman named Dorine, took them regularly throughout the fall and spring when they were in the second and third grades. All of them were precocious children, and the trip was always an adventure. There was the grouchy duck who barked at them: "That duck barked at me," shouted Warren. "Ducks don't bark, ducks quack," shouted back White Mike. "Yes, Michael," said Dorine, who was paid $350 a week. And then she started making quacking noises that sent the boys into peals of laughter.

The boys liked the monkeys too ("Are they throwing their poop? Dory, are they throwing their poop?") and the penguins and the seals, and really all the animals they saw, even the snakes.

The trip picked up rituals. No matter what time it was, they would always wait till the next half hour to leave so they could see the clock with the animal statues strike the time.

But the most important ritual, the one that the boys remembered for as long as they lived, was the buying of popguns. The man who sold popguns and plastic swords and balloons from his cart was dark and had a mustache, and once Hunter asked him if he was a pirate, and he said yes. Every week the boys would get new popguns, and the popguns would always break by Thursday, usually because the strings attaching the corks to the barrel would become inextricably tangled in the firing mechanism. Dorine made it clear to the boys that she would not spend her afternoons fixing popguns, and if they broke, too bad. You must take care of your things.

It fell to White Mike, then, to fix the popguns. He was the best at it, had the most patience for the intricacies of the tangled strings. So Warren and Hunter and Charlie would shoot one another bang dead with the popguns, and then they would argue over whose gun was whose when the first one broke, and then White Mike would try to fix them.

Years later, when White Mike was walking in the park, he looked for the man who sold the popguns. He couldn't find the cart or the man, and he realized that, in fact, he had not seen a popgun in years. He realized that he hadn't seen Dorine in years either, and he wondered what had happened to her and if Warren still had her phone number. White Mike started imagining what he would say if he spoke with her.

That he was seventeen now and he got it, he saw how the adult world was working, and he was sorry he'd been a little shit as a kid. That he got her job and that he remembered being taken to the zoo, and thanks for that because she didn't really have to do it; and it is a good thing you were there to raise me and Warren and Charlie and Hunter, because if you hadn't, I might be like one of those kids I sell to, and do you smoke dope?

Yes, Michael, she might say, at those parties, me and all the other nannies and housekeepers used to smoke spliffs out in the back stairwell and talk about the famous beautiful people at the party after I put you to sleep. And don't you know, Michael, that we really moved like ghosts in and out of all your lives, just the way the good help should.

Yeah, I know, Dory. It's like what I do now, this dealing, it's like that. I move in and out like a ghost, so no one remembers when I'm gone. It is the way the best help is supposed to be.

Yes, Michael, but we had fun at the zoo with Charlie and Warren and Hunter and the Grouchy Duck, didn't we? Remember when the duck barked at Charlie?

Ducks don't bark, Dory, they quack.

# 18

JESSICA GETS UP at eleven, barely remembering that Chris put her in a cab and told the driver where she lived. She remembers her doorman helping her, though that doesn't matter now because it is almost noon and she feels really shitty, but she has a date with some of her girlfriends to go ice-skating. She hangs around with these three girls all the time, even though she knows she is much smarter than they are. They agree about certain fundamental things, and this holds them together. They agree about who is cool and who is not. They agree that it is okay to give blow jobs but not to have sex until, like, the time is right. They agree that they should never have to buy their own drinks at bars. They agree that chicks must come before dicks. They agree that they are all sexy, but each more so than the other three. They agree that the Hamptons rock and that their parents suck, *even though, like, I tell my mom everything, but not everything everything, you know?* So the four of them are going ice-skating this morning, and they meet at Wollman Rink in Central Park. They wear tight blue jeans and ribbed sweaters and parkas and nice gloves. They all have good skin and are pretty. They treat guys badly, but the guys don't care, as long as they can get maybe a blow job once in a while. Everyone knows exactly what is going on.

As they put on their skates, the girls talk about how they are repulsed by the sweet smell of nachos and fake cheese, popcorn and hot dogs. This is not their kind of food. But, alas, none of them has her own skating rink, at least not in the city. Arm in arm, they head out onto the ice. They giggle as they go.

*Like, like, like, like, like, like . . .*

*Like, no way.*

Three times around and the girls are ready to get off the ice when a gawky kid skating by himself slips and falls in front of them. The girls try to veer out of the way, but Jessica is unable to make it. And one of her skates cuts across the boy's forehead, just under his bangs. He yells in pain and then clutches his head. Blood swirls out on the ice, and the girls all scream as they race for the edge of the rink. The boy pushes his hand on the cut to stop the bleeding. His name is Andrew. He wouldn't have been here to begin with, but he made this plan with his friend Hunter, who can skate like a hockey player. Then he got that crazy call from Hunter about jail, and his father went down there but told Andrew he couldn't come. So Andrew decided to go skating anyway. People always say Andrew is a little distracted. Ice-skating without girls? Just on his own? Guy's probably gay.

# 19

THE SKATING GIRLS are like so totally freaked out that they have to go and have a hot chocolate together at Jackson Hole. But once they all hit Fifth Avenue, Jessica heads in a different direction. She has to make a call.

"Hello?"

"Chris, it's Jessica. Thanks for taking care of me last night."

"Sure, yeah." Chris isn't surprised. He helped her when she was passed out, and didn't try to fuck her or anything.

"I mean it," she says. She wants some more of whatever she had the night before. The high was the best thing she's ever felt. And now it's faded and gone. And some more would be good, before vacation is over. Just another taste before she has to go back to school. She doesn't need much or anything. Just a *little* more. She walks faster. She is sweating under her parka.

"You get your weed from that White Mike guy, right?"

"Yeah."

"Could I get his number?"

"Yeah, sure. You wanna get some and smoke?"

"Actually, no, I wanted to get something else."

"Coke?" Chris won't do coke. His brother, Claude, used to do a ton, and it fucked Claude up. Chris doesn't know what to tell Jessica about all that.

"No, what I did last night."

"I thought you were drunk."

"No, it's like coke but more like Ecstasy." Jessica is speaking very quickly. The words tumble over one another. "Then it was like something totally different."

"What was it?"

"I don't know, it was just called *Twelve*."

# 20

ANDREW MAKES it off the ice with blood dripping down his face. The rink manager calls an ambulance, and at Lenox Hill Hospital, a doctor stitches him up but says he has to stay for observation for six hours, because the stitches are so close to his eye. They put him in a room on the third floor with another kid. The two hit it off and are happy for company as they lie there, stoned.

Actually, neither is really happy for company. They are happy that they are rooming with another private school white kid who doesn't smell. It could be a lot worse. Especially for Andrew, who can tell the other kid is on much heavier drugs than he is.

That girl Sara Ludlow comes to visit. Her boyfriend is the other kid, Sean: *captain of the football team, skier at Vail, brown hair, born in the hospital he now lies in, school on Seventy-third Street, father on Wall Street, mother just chauffeured back to Eighty-fourth Street, whatever*—this kid is very high. *And who obeys the street signs anyway.*

Sean was in a car accident coming back from East Hampton in the new PT Cruiser his parents bought him for Christmas. Sara gives Andrew the once-over as she comes in, then looks at Sean's IV and kisses him on the forehead.

"Ohh, how are you? How's your arm?"

"I don't know."

Andrew is watching and listening from the other bed. He is pretending to be half asleep as he takes in Sara's beauty. She is wearing tight jeans and has her hair in a ponytail. Andrew is horny.

"Where are your parents?" she asks Sean.

"Came and went."

"So what do the doctors say?"

"I don't even know."

"You must be on pretty heavy drugs, huh?"

"Yeah."

"Can I have some?"

"No, those are for when I go home." Sean sounds suddenly angry.

"It was a joke," she says.

Andrew laughs, and Sara turns to him but can't seem to decide whether to smile or scowl. She does both. Sean drifts off.

"Sorry. I'm Andrew."

"Sara."

"Sara Ludlow."

"You know me?" as if everybody doesn't. In fact, Sara knows she is famous. She likes being famous. She wants to be more famous. Here's how you do it. First you're famous in your grade, then you're famous in your school. Then you're famous in all the schools, and then in the city, or at least the part of the city that matters. And then you've got a career.

"Do you know that girl Vanessa who goes to your school?" He asks.

"Yeah."

"She's friends with my sister."

"Everybody knows everybody." She can hear he has the Dave Matthews Band's *Under the Table and Dreaming* in his Discman, and she likes that music. "I've been meaning to get that album," she says.

"You wanna take this one?"

"No, I couldn't . . ."

"No, really, take it." *Excuse to see her again,* Andrew thinks, *and Dave Matthews blows anyway.* "Yeah, I've got other CDs. You can give it back to me next time I see you."

"That's sweet. Thanks a lot."

"I'll find you through him." He nods at the other bed.

"Okay, great."

"All right, I'm leaving, okay?" she says, looking at Sean.

"What about football?" he asks.

"What did the doctor say?"

"I might be out, I don't remember."

"Good. Okay. Bye-bye."

Sara walks for the door. Andrew watches the perfect smoothness of the denim on the back of her thighs as she walks away. After a while, he goes back to thinking about Hunter. There is not much he can do, he decides, but think. His father said he couldn't just call all the ritzy hotels in Europe. It would take time. Hunter didn't even know which country his parents were in when he talked to Andrew on the phone.

# 21

*WHITE MIKE AND his father moved right after his mother died of breast cancer, three and a half years ago. It was hot in the new place, and there was nothing on the walls. In his room, there were bookcases and there were books on them and that was good, but everything else was stacked haphazardly, and the big box of his old stuff was sticking out of the closet so he could see it. Maybe you know how it is and maybe you don't, but sometimes if you can't see what you're finished with, it's better. The room was big, but getting rid of the box seemed to clear up a lot of space. White Mike stripped to his shorts and lay down on the floor, spread-eagling his body, so he felt a little cooler. That's how it was for him that first night in his new room.*

# 22

WHEN SHE LEAVES Lenox Hill, Sara walks over to Madison. She takes her Nokia phone out of her Prada bag hanging over her black North Face parka. No missed calls. She accesses the menu and scrolls down until she comes to a new entry from last night: *Chris*. She has a plan. She hits the talk.

"Hello?"

"Are you with anybody?"

"No. Who's this?"

"Can I come over?"

"Sure, yeah. I mean, who are you?"

"Me. Sara. I'm coming over."

Chris is very surprised and very happy. Yesterday he thought she didn't even know who he was. Now she has his phone number and everything. Maybe she has everybody's phone number. Probably. Anyway, she's coming over.

Sara walks up the steps of Chris's town house and presses the button on the intercom. Chris's voice comes across. Sara announces herself. Chris says hold on. She gets in.

It's Saturday, so the house is empty except for Chris and Claude. Sara wishes she could get rid of the housekeeper and her little brother's nanny when her parents are away, which is always. She has to ask Chris how he does it. She can tell a lot of people work in this house. Sara follows Chris up to his room on the fourth floor. A television is buzzing and moaning in some corner. Chris is wearing basketball shorts, white and black, and Kevin Garnett sneakers—the ones that zip up the top. He is also wearing a wife beater, but he is not particularly beef, so it sort of hangs on him and brings out the pale skin and pimples on his hairless chest. *Chacne* is the name for pimples on the chest; *bacne*, the name for pimples on the back. Chris hopes she doesn't notice and sits down on one of the couches in his room and stretches out his arms on the back. His armpit hair is sparse. Jessica sits in the thousand-dollar black and gray swivel chair opposite him. Chris gets up and goes to his computer, where he starts the first song on his playlist. The first song is Tupac Shakur's "California Love."

Sara smiles at him. "Listen, I have this great idea."

"Okay."

"Your parents aren't going to be here for a few days, right?"

"Yeah."

"We should throw a party."

"What about last night?"

"No, I mean a real party."

Chris doesn't know what to say. She's just so beautiful.

"I could get everybody to come," she says. "Everybody cool."

"I don't want it to be too big."

Sara is not in the mood for this. She gets up and sits down close to Chris on the couch. He tenses, surprised by the arm she places around his shoulders.

*I can't believe I'm doing this,* thinks Sara, mockingly, to herself. *I am trading on my womanly wiles for something I want. Ha, ha.* She slips her tongue into Chris's mouth. He reciprocates, and with perfect timing, she pulls away.

"Don't you want to have a big party?"

"Sure." His dick is getting stiff and visible through his Jordan shorts.

"The biggest party ever," she says. "It'll be amazing." She knows the right party on New Year's Eve will lock her in as the girl who makes things happen. Which everyone knows she is already, but this would still be great. Great. Great for her.

"Just not too many people."

"But it has to be huge. Besides, people will need to keep themselves occupied in case we start to have some extra fun, by ourselves, somewhere else." Sara glances meaningfully at the bed.

"I thought you had a boyfriend."

"I have lots of boyfriends," she says, smiling at him. "That's the way it works. I'm not a slut—"

"Of course you're not."

"But different guys are interesting for different reasons. There are just so many of you. You're interesting for a very specific reason."

"What's that?"

"You'll have to figure that out for yourself."

\*   \*   \*

*Sara's grandmother went to a coming-out party once that was supposed to be the most famous party of her generation. It was out on Long Island. Not in the Hamptons, but on the North Shore where they used to have huge estates with incredible gardens on the Sound. This party was so wild, kids really were swinging from chandeliers, and the place got totally trashed. Cops came from two counties, and eight or nine boys from Yale and Columbia were arrested. The story was on the cover of* Life *magazine. Sara's mother was born nine months later.*

# 23

WHITE MIKE IS walking down Lexington toward Ninety-first Street to meet Jessica. He is with Lionel, because when he got the call, he knew he would need this new Twelve stuff. The girl had described the drug perfectly when she was asking for it, even though she had asked for "The Number Twelve." He knew what it was. It was practically like she was still on it.

The whole deal is starting to make White Mike uneasy. This new drug is bad news. Plus, he is having to deal with Lionel all the time because of it, and Lionel is a creepy dude. Lionel with his brown and yellow bloodshot eyes. White Mike knows that Lionel carries a gun. The gun is the scariest thing that goes along with making more money. White Mike never saw a gun in the beginning, but pretty soon the money got more serious. Once a thousand dollars is changing hands, the dealers always have some kind of protection. It is just too much money to fuck around with. The kids, of course, have no idea.

Intellectually, White Mike knows everything. He knows that Lionel comes from a place where there actually was crack, even if there's not so much anymore. He knows that Lionel's neighborhood can get really fucked up, manifest the specter of the inner city he and all his friends heard about in history class but only White Mike ever came close to seeing. White Mike is *cognizant* of, even involved in, this other New York City. All of which makes it weird and not weird at the same time that he knows, say, that Lionel has children. And get this: Lionel told him how in the third grade his son, Jeremy, had been disciplined by a teacher for writing on his desk, and the kid had said, *My dad's gonna shoot you.* The teacher backed off, then quit later that year. Lionel was proud of that: *Sure, I'd have shot the bitch. Shoot any bitch-ass nigger fucks with me. Teacher, cop, punk kid, doesn't matter to me. All the same anyway.* The words stuck in White Mike's head. White Mike and Lionel don't talk as they walk.

As they get to Ninety-first, they see Jessica waiting on the corner, walking around a phone booth. She keeps looking around but doesn't notice the two drug dealers until they are almost right on top of her. She is trying to play it cool, but she has never done this before. White Mike feels sorry for her.

Lionel eyes the girl, but she is focusing her attention on White Mike. He is the one she can deal with. They introduce themselves, and White Mike inquires as to how much she wants. First, though, Jessica wants to know exactly what the stuff is called, even though she doesn't want to come off as naïve. So she braces herself and asks, looking away from White Mike. Lionel grins and grunts with laughter.

"Twelve," White Mike says. He tries to look her right in the eye but can't catch her gaze.

"Sorry?"

"*Twelve.*"

"Oh."

Lionel's baritone slides out from his hood, surprisingly smooth, even musical. "How much," he says, not even really a question.

For the first time, Jessica really looks at him. The dark skin hooded under the sweatshirt, unwashed, and the eyes looking straight at her. Lionel is handsome, in his way. He has a strong jaw and doesn't look fat, even though he is enormous. Jessica takes this all in.

"A thousand." She almost totally busted her cash-advance lines for this.

Lionel's eyebrows arch for half a second. White Mike sighs and indicates for the three of them to start walking, and takes the money from the girl, crisp bills in his hand, and Lionel hands her five tiny Baggies. Jessica now has the impression that this drug is Lionel's domain and not White Mike's. Her attention is refocused. White Mike is surprised when she asks Lionel for his beeper number, "because, you know, it might be easier if it was direct, and maybe I'll want some more. . . ."

Lionel gives her the number. White Mike doesn't want to think about this.

Jessica, eager to get away from them now, says good-bye and turns the corner hurrying toward Fifth Avenue.

*That was easy.*

*I am so cool.*

# 24

WHITE MIKE LOOKED *at her as she spoke. His mother said that it could be a couple years, but it might be less, and at the end she said she was sorry, and he said, Don't worry, it's not your fault. She said she wasn't going to talk about it anymore, and they were just going to live the best life they could. Did you hear me, Michael? Always live the best life you can.*

*That night White Mike woke up sometime after midnight and walked to the kitchen in the dark. There were no windows in the old kitchen, and when the swinging door swooshed silently closed behind him, the room was black. Not even a sliver of light came through the crack under the door. He reached up to a cupboard, opened it, and searched for a package of cookies. His hands found the package and took it down, all in total darkness. Next he pulled a stool up to the cupboard to get a glass. The first thing he felt was a champagne flute, so he took that, and it was as cold as the tiles on his bare feet. He placed the glass next to the package of cookies on the counter. He opened the package as silently as he could and removed a stack of cookies, the whole bunch in* the first of the divided rows of the package. He placed the stack next to the flute, closed up the package, and replaced it in the cupboard. He turned in the direction of the refrigerator and regarded the darkness before him. Then he closed his eyes, and the darkness changed imperceptibly, maybe just in that he knew his eyes were closed. He stepped across the kitchen to the refrigerator and opened the door. Orange brightness flooded his closed eyes, and he reached about for the carton of milk. He found a carton, cold and full, and took it out, closing the door as quickly as he could. The brightness faded, and he opened his eyes. In the darkness he opened the carton and poured himself a champagne flute of undiluted cranberry juice, his mother's favorite drink.

# 25

WHITE MIKE AND Lionel watch the girl hurry away.

"We'll be seeing that one again soon," says Lionel.

"You seen my cousin?" White Mike asks.

"Who?" Lionel is thumbing the cash.

"You know, Charlie. He put us together. Goes to college now. Still deals."

Lionel thinks back to the feathers flying up in front of his eyes as the parka exploded under Charlie's face. The other kid flashes through his mind too, down on the pavement.

"Oh, yeah."

"If you see him, tell him I'm looking for him."

"Yeah." Lionel peaces himself out and walks off quickly, to go back uptown and get stoned.

"Fucking guy," White Mike is muttering under his breath as he catches a cab.

*Where is Charlie?* Charlie has been on White Mike's mind a lot recently. He grew up with the kid, after all. Charlie is his cousin. His father's sister is Charlie's mother. But she and her husband were all fucked up. Way too much money, in the gossip columns all the time, party-party-party, and it was houses in Tuscany and chartered boats off Bali. Their family is much wealthier than White Mike's father. For most of Charlie's life, it was either live with the nannies or live with White Mike. So Charlie just used his parents' house when he wanted to throw a party or something. He kept that address, but he really lived with White Mike. They were almost the same age and looked like brothers; people used to mistake them for twins. The big difference between them was that Charlie was a very bad student, or just didn't care, or both, and was sent away to a bad boarding school in eighth grade. It made him grow up faster, in a funny way.

White Mike always looked forward to Charlie's return during vacations: it always brought interesting adventures and eventually tutorials in drug dealing. When Charlie came back home this time, though, he was different. Maybe it was the new school, or maybe it was just that he was doing more drugs than usual—college didn't stop that—but he had been distant. Like his mind was on something. He went off without White Mike for basically the whole vacation; doing what, White Mike couldn't guess. So the hell with Charlie. The whole deal is making White Mike cranky.

# 26

JESSICA STRUTS DOWN Fifth Avenue, anticipating, her high, shapely ass swinging and hair flying, beautiful in the light streaming through the sky at the tail end of dusk. She takes her purple Discman out of her bag and puts on the headphones, the kind that wrap around the back of your neck. She is listening to a mix a boy made for her. Jessica walks on, hand in her pocket, fondling the tiny Baggies.

# 27

"WHY DON'T YOU do drugs? You deal 'em; why don't you do 'em?" asked Hunter as he handed White Mike the bong disguised as a highlighter that he bought in a smoke shop downtown.

White Mike looked at it and handed it back. "I don't know. I just never had the urge to."

"Not even to try?"

"No."

# 28

WHITE MIKE IS thinking about Charlie again. About the time when, as usual, his cousin's parents were out of town and he wanted to cut school and fly down to Florida. It wasn't even spring break, but Charlie and a couple of buddies were going to stay in some resort in Key West and get shitfaced and laid all the time.

Charlie routinely took thousands of dollars from the checking account his father kept to run the house. His father knew this, of course, but kept putting more money in. There was no lack of it. This time, for some reason, there wasn't enough money to cover the plane tickets.

But Charlie really wanted to take the trip, and his mother had some expensive jewelry, so he went into the safe in her dressing room and took this one necklace and pawned it to a jewelry guy he found who had a kind of storefront shop over on Ninth Avenue in the Fifties. Charlie pawned the necklace for twelve grand. While Charlie was at the shop, he saw that the place discreetly traded in guns too. He told all his buddies, and so the place became the place where you could get guns. The

shop was called Angela's Pawn shop, though no one knew any
Angela. So kids would go in and ask to see the guns sometimes,
but never buy them. Except for Charlie. He was really proud
of the gun he bought there.

The next day Charlie was on the plane (first class) with
his boys listening to Nelly on his Discman . . .

> *Can I make it?*
> *Damn right*
> *I be on the next flight*
> *Paying cash*
> *First class*
> *Sittin' next to Vanna White*

. . . when his mother came back from France and became hys-
terical after realizing that her necklace was missing. She called
the insurance company and fired the maid and hired a private
investigator. By the time Charlie got back from Florida, a police report had been filed, and an insurance claim for $175,000
was about to go through. It was at this point that White Mike
explained to Charlie how serious this was and talked him into
telling his mother what he had done. That was a scene, but in
the end Charlie told his mother where the jewelry was, and she
went and got it back, and they all wound up being investigated
for insurance fraud. Charlie was sent briefly to some boot camp
in Montana for bad rich kids. He learned to ride horses there.

*Charlie said he loved the gun because of how shiny it was when it
fit in your hand. It was like pointing lightning. White Mike took*

*the little silver gun in his hand and sighted along the barrel, aiming it at Charlie's head. White Mike told Charlie that he didn't like the gun, and handed it back, and they didn't talk about that anymore. Instead, they talked about cowboys. The way they wore their guns slung low, with the holsters open and the trigger guards cut away so that when the bad guy arrived at high noon, you could pull your iron before he could, and in the end he would fall to the ground and you would still be standing. And Charlie said it was really about how fast you pulled your gun, and White Mike said, No, Charlie, it's really about pulling the trigger.*

# 29

TOBIAS HAS A Saturday meeting at his agency. Tobias has been a part-time model since getting discovered on the beach in East Hampton when he was eleven. His father wants him to go to Princeton, but Tobias wants to be a full-time model after high school. No way will he get into Princeton anyway, but father keeps saying he'll take care of it. Whatever.

Tobias remembers the first time he saw himself on the side of a bus in a Guess jeans ad. The utter euphoria, the elation, of seeing the lady at the bus stop double-take between him and the ad. Tobias was hooked. And at the shoots there were hands touching his head and face and body, styling, primping, caressing; he loved every minute of it. Being posed by the photographer and hearing the click of the shutter, and then, however long later, taking the picture and cropping and gluing it with surgical care in his leather-bound scrapbook with his initials embossed in gold on the spine. Tobias has been thinking that he might want to get a tattoo of his initials embossed in gold on his own spine, a couple inches above his ass, at his center of gravity.

When he gets to the waiting room, there is a beautiful girl sitting in one of the chairs. This is not surprising—she is, of course, a model. Tobias thinks how much he would like to sleep with this particular girl.

# 30

HER NAME IS Molly.

Molly is sixteen. She wears her jeans baggy over her thin legs, ankles crossed all the way at the bottom of those legs, so far from her head, the low-top black Nikes over sockless feet. Her brown hair is tied up, and her glasses rest on the tip of her nose, freckled and perhaps sharper than fashionable, but an undeniably exquisite asset to her face. Thin eyebrows react subtly as she reads, furrowing, caterpillaring, and cocking above her liquid eyes. The gray turtleneck sweater hangs loose over her obviously curvy torso. Little bits of fluff and strands of wool catch the sunlight as bands of it come through the blinds, more white than yellow, and crisscross her chest and the tip of her chin. She is reading *Ragtime* by E. L. Doctorow, and she likes it very much.

Tobias has never read *Ragtime*. He has read the latest issue of *Maxim*, however, and has learned several things from it. First, how to make a Lava lamp. Second, that to get a girl in bed, you shouldn't act interested. Or rather, you should act interested but not too interested. Keep 'em guessing. Tobias couldn't keep a paper bag guessing, and Molly, by all rights, should not have been interested in him. But Tobias is handsome, and Molly is a little confused.

Molly's parents come from the land of crazy people. Or maybe the land of assholes. Molly was in a health class at her school one day, and the teacher was talking about the importance of role models. Molly, uncharacteristically, raised her hand. She was by nature a quiet girl. She asked the teacher: "Okay, but what happens when the people who are supposed to be role models are jerks?"

The teacher replied: "I don't think I understand the question."

Molly thought: *No kidding.*

*The spring break of her eighth-grade year, the beautiful Molly went on a trip with her crazy parents to visit with some of her father's friends who had rented a compound on Scotsman's Cay in the Bahamas. Molly doesn't remember how they were all connected, but there were several families and lots of kids. The second oldest was a boy named Mike whose mother was sick and didn't come. Molly had a crush on him, but she knew nothing would ever come of it because he was, like, a family friend and that never worked.*

*The thing that made the trip bad for Molly, though, was not an unrequited crush. It was that her father said he had some sort of infection on his thigh so he couldn't go snorkeling. He would just hang around the house all day, making phone calls and wait-*

*ing for everyone to get back so he could drink his wine with them. The truth was that he was a bad athlete and a bad swimmer and didn't want to go on any adventures where people would see that. So he would drop hints about his pain, and go on and on about how sorry he was that he was missing out on so much.*

*White Mike noticed how she felt and told her to concentrate on what she saw underwater. He said it worked for him, so it would work for her too.*

# 31

TOBIAS MAKES CONVERSATION with Molly. He seems like a kid from the other crowd. A kid who gets fucked up and goes to those open houses that Molly always hears stories about afterward. He is sort of glamorous, even. Tobias tells her about his recent trek through Chinatown, and how he got some new pets—a tank of piranhas. Molly listens and tells him she likes fish and animals and has a sheepdog named Thomas—which is not true. She doesn't want him to figure her out. She tries to be a little different. She puts down *Ragtime* so he can't see the cover.

They talk about how hard it is to be a model until Tobias gets called inside. She gets called in before he's out, but after her meeting, he is there waiting for her.

"I thought if you were still here, you might want to come and see the piranhas."

"Sure," Molly says. *Here we go*.

Tobias has been keeping his flesh-eating icythiopods at Claude's house, to Claude's delight. They are living in a neon-lit

phosphorescent-blue aquarium above the bed in the guest bedroom with the drums on the fifth floor, across from Claude's
room and the balcony. Molly is wary of her surroundings. She
is certainly not intimidated by the splendor of the house, but
her apartment is pretty small by comparison. Everyone is
wealthy, but there are gradations.

Tobias turns off the lights, and the aquarium glows blue.

Molly hears the sounds of professional wrestling. Claude
is watching television in his bedroom across the hall. The faux
violence is rendered in astonishing digital clarity on the flat-
screen television hanging on the wall like a painting. That room
is in the dark too, and when Tobias and Molly step in to say
hello, Claude swivels his head and squints angrily at the light
coming through the door. Tobias introduces Molly. Claude
doesn't mute the wrestling and has nothing to say, so after the
introduction, Tobias takes Molly back to the piranha room. He
has seen Claude's weirdness before. Molly is silent.

Tobias asks her if she wants to see something cool. She
says yeah. He says to wait here. He goes down to the kitchen
and opens the refrigerator. He removes a half-eaten rotisserie-
cooked chicken, flaky and dull golden and cold, the bones pro-
truding. He brings it back upstairs and tells Molly to watch this.
He drops the chicken into the tank and presses the timer button on his digital watch.

One: the fish rip at the flesh, and there is no blood, but
the organic matter is shredded, and some rises to the surface
as the fish dart at the main body.

Two: hunks of the meat seemingly disappear, and Molly
starts as one of the fish rams the chicken corpse violently into
the glass.

Three: the meat is gone, and the bones float around the tank trailing bits of vestigial chicken flesh.

"Cool, huh?"

"Yeah, uh, wow."

Molly says she has to leave. Tobias says come to the big open house in two days, for New Year's Eve. Molly has no plans for New Year's Eve. She has never been to an open house. She says she will come, thinking she can get out of it anytime. She realizes that the whole time she has been with Tobias, she hasn't really said anything. On her way out, she does say hi to Chris, whose peach-fuzzed jaw drops when he sees her in his house.

# 32

THE FORENSIC TESTS have identified the blood on Hunter's clothing. It is Nana's.

In the holding cell, Hunter is playing Friday night over and over in his head. He is trying to remember an alibi, some proof of where he was. The receipt for his doughnuts has the time printed on it, but it was hours too late. But what kind of a murderer goes and buys jelly doughnuts four hours after he kills? *Probably all of them,* thinks Hunter. None of that matters.

There was that one thing last night, though. Hunter remembers the old con man. Some old guy with crooked teeth and a ragged suit. He was tall, actually, huge, four or five inches taller than Hunter. And he leaned down right into Hunter's face and said something about a hospital and his friend and coffee and could Hunter give him just a couple dollars right now. Hunter asked if the money was for a cab to the hospital, and it was then that the man started crying. This giant, crazy old man with a scruffy face and crooked teeth started crying and repeating *Two dollars, two dollars, two dollars,* sometimes speaking English and sometimes some other language. More crying. It reminded Hunter of his father.

# 33

EVERYONE SAID *White Mike looked handsome in the dark suit he wore to his mother's funeral. He didn't care. There was a wig on his mother's corpse, which made him angry. Wigs weren't real, and he wanted real. He would have rather seen her for the last time with her head bald.*

# 34

CHRIS IS ANNOYED at having to come downstairs and sign for everything when the UPS truck arrives. He was watching TV. The delivery guys have about ten boxes, and he tells them to put them in the wrapping room, down the hall from the front door and to the left. He misses the look they give him when he says *wrapping room*. It is there that Chris's mother keeps gifts, and the necessary tape and ribbons and paper.

When the delivery guys are gone, Chris takes a steak knife from the kitchen and opens one of the boxes and pulls out a smaller box and opens it. It is a brass bell, flawlessly cast and with names engraved on it:

> *Jeff and Trina*
> *Happy New Year*

Chris holds it by the handle and flicks his wrist. A high clear note rings out in the silence of the house.

He looks through the boxes and finds more bells of different sizes with other people's names engraved on them. He comes to the realization that his mother's better friends, the people she is more interested in having as friends, get the bigger bells. He pulls out a big one and rings it with the smaller one and hears the deeper tones echo through the house. He can hold only one in each hand, but he takes out a dozen of them and lines them up on the wrapping table, then starts picking them up and playing them two at a time until he is in a frenzy and the big house is ringing with the sound of bells. And then his arms are tired and he lets the last note ring out and when it fades away finally, after a minute or two (for they are well-made bells), Chris heads upstairs to the television to kill the hours before he has to go to a cocktail party at his aunt's house with his brother. It is one of their obligations, instead of taking out the garbage, maybe.

# 35

WHITE MIKE WAS *a thinker, his teachers said. This is what he was thinking as he watched his mother's coffin being lowered into the ground.*

*You will not be remembered if you die now. You will be buried and mourned by a few, and what more can you ask for. But you feel so tremendously alone, because you fear that your blood is not strong or good and your friends are few and embattled too. But so what. That is the answer. So what so what so what so what so what so what so what. The world will spiral out from underneath you, and you will find nothing to hold on to because you are either too smart or too dumb to find God, and because what the fuck will Camus ever do for you? Just ideas. You are not an artist, you will not leave something behind. Maybe you are angry only because the way out is through love and you are horny and lonely. And she's dead, of course. Maybe this is the way it is for everybody, only you are weaker, or less lucky, or have seen something they all have not. You have seen that before you lies a great stretch of road, and it is windswept or blasted by the hot sun or covered in snow, or it is dirt or concrete or shrouded in darkness or bright and clear so you have to squint, but no matter what, it is utterly empty.*

*That was what White Mike was thinking.*

# 36

CHRIS AND CLAUDE smoke a joint together before they go to the cocktail party. They don't do this very often, smoke together, and it feels weird to both of them, but what the fuck.

Auntie lives in a huge prewar duplex way over on the Upper West Side. The rooms are crowded, loud, and smoky. Short Chicana women in black and white servers' uniforms carry trays with salmon on toast, little piles of sushi, tiny kabobs, and other miniature food.

Chris and Claude stand together in a corner. They have snatched a whole plate of salmon sandwiches and are eating greedily, if discreetly. Occasionally they are pulled along somewhere by Auntie, who wants to introduce them to someone. They cannot wait to get back home where there are no adults. Claude does tequila shots because no one will bother him about it. Chris thinks about what the older women might look like naked.

At one point, Auntie drags Chris and Claude over to meet Marcelle, a middle-aged friend of their mother. Marcelle is an unpublished novelist. She prides herself on being hip. Up-to-date. There are lots of adults like this. Marcelle asks Chris what kind of music he listens to. He, in order to extricate himself, responds, "Oh, you know, everything."

"What do you think about Eminem?" Marcelle persists.

"I think he is a great MC," says Chris, "and he can say what he wants to say."

"Oh, I agree, I absolutely love his album."

"Which one?"

Marcelle doesn't miss a beat. "Oh, you know, the new one. But you know," she moves on quickly, "you can learn a lot from music."

"Of course," agrees Chris.

Marcelle smiles. "Now, I'm not religious really. Everything I believe, *my* philosophy, is in the song 'Imagine.' You know, by John and Yoko?"

"You a Beatles fan?" asks Chris.

"Yeah, they're great artists."

"Fuck the Beatles," says Claude.

# 37

BY MIDNIGHT Jessica has done all the Twelve she was saving for New Year's Eve. *Shit,* she thinks, when she wakes up later and her sheets are damp with sweat.

# 38

THE KID White Mike sells to is handsome, like a model, wearing shorts and flip-flops, like it's summer and he has just stepped out of his house for a second to pay for pizza or something. He reminds White Mike of the summer he worked at a camp on the eastern tip of Long Island. It was the last summer before his father sold the house in Amagansett. White Mike and a girl named Alice would hang out behind the boathouse, the spot where everyone went to smoke. Alice was the smartest girl, the girl who was up for anything. She was a pack-a-day smoker. White Mike didn't smoke. He just went behind the boathouse to be with Alice, who would sit cross-legged against the wall, and smoke and tease him. He was not yet White Mike.

*"First kiss," Alice said, "first time I tried weed, first time I got drunk, first time I drove, first boyfriend, dumping of first boyfriend. First time I had sex. I remember the dates of all my firsts. Don't you?"*
  *"Just some."*

*"Why don't you drink?"*
*"I don't know," said White Mike.*
*"Existential crisis," she said. "Read* The Plague.*"*


White Mike comes out of the memory as he is passing the huge Barnes & Noble on Eighty-sixth Street. When he walks in, the colors are bright, and upstairs there are people drinking coffee while they read. White Mike runs his hands along every shelf of books he passes, feeling the texture beneath his fingers. When he gets to the Literature section, he searches for *C*, and when he finds it, he kneels down and looks for Camus and then for *The Plague,* which he buys in hardcover.

In bed later, he reads again about the death of the rats.

# 39

CLAUDE WANTS TO go out after the cocktail party. He calls
Tobias on his cell phone and tells him to come over, enticing
him with weed. Tobias tells Claude that he just scored some
weed from that pale dealer in the overcoat, but he'll put on some
pants and come over anyway. Claude has no intention of smoking. He wants to stay clear headed. He just wants Tobias for
the company, sort of, while he goes downtown. Claude knows
exactly where he is going. Back to the part of Chinatown where
he bought the weapons. They are somehow just not enough.
There has to be something else.

The two of them, tall and hooded, get off the subway at
Spring Street and walk to Mulberry. Soon the smells of hot duck
and rabbit flesh and cold fish are floating out in the night. When
Claude gets to the next corner, he stops in front of the first store
he went into the night before. Tobias is lagging behind a little
bit, and Claude decides that he no longer wants the company.
He doesn't say anything and hurries along the street and down
an alley. He peeks back out around the corner and watches a

confused Tobias call his name and then swing his fist and yell "Fuck!" and then wander off up the street. When Tobias is gone, Claude emerges from the darkness and walks into the store.

The tiny, fat woman is not behind the counter; instead, a short, wrinkled old man. He and Claude are the only people in the store. He looks at Claude and says, "Yes?" Claude wants to know if any "special products" are being sold.

The man looks at Claude for a long second, then says, "Wait." Then he walks to the front door, locks it, and goes into the back room. Claude doesn't expect much. The man returns with something cloth-wrapped that he sets on the counter. He removes the cloth and reveals an Uzi, black and oiled but worn down, looking, to Claude, like something straight out of the movies.

# 40

WHITE MIKE FALLS asleep with his light on and *The Plague* on his chest.

He dreams of skyscrapers. He dreams that he is high on the roof of one and there is a thunderstorm raging around him. The girders under his feet sway and rock in the wind, and forked lightning shoots silently down into the city, and then thunder explodes in his ears. The city is bright and loud, but he is alone at the top of this swaying building, and as it begins to rain he walks to the edge of the building to get a good look at the rest of the city and watch the lightning come down, and in a great flash of white he knows that his building has been struck and he feels himself up and flying over the railing, then falling down through the air. He can see himself flailing on the way down and feel his stomach float up in his body, and in his sleep he kicks out and flails his arms but doesn't wake up. And he keeps falling and falling and at the end he sees himself land on a car, on his side, and he sees the roof flatten. He watches his body, in overcoat and jeans, from afar as his view tracks out as if it were the final scene in a movie, and the raindrops splatter the crushed metal around his body.

# 41

GHOST OF *Christmas Past. White Mike was walking down the beach in East Hampton on Christmas break, and he was listening to Alice —whom he had run into out there—tell him about her parents, and boarding school, and everything else. It was all bad. Then it was getting dark and cold. What she did next was take off her clothes and run into the ocean. She came out laughing and crying and freezing to death all at the same time.*

# Part III
# Sunday, December 29

# 42

"I THINK I know why you don't drink," said Alice. They were in a bar on Second Avenue that served kids. She was drinking a cosmopolitan; he was drinking coffee.

"Why?" asked White Mike.

"You like the power you have from being sober all the time around people who are fucked up."

# 43

CHRIS IS HAVING a boxing lesson in the morning sunlight that falls through the windows of the library in his town house. It is an odd place for a boxing lesson, but the coach wants to have it in that room so he can look at the books while the kid works out.

For Chris's seventeenth birthday, his father called a gym on Thirteenth Street and hired a coach to teach his son how to box. They went down to the gym together. Chris had been scared in the gym, of the dirt and the grime and all the strong dudes beating the shit out of the bags and each other. In the car on the way back uptown, he convinced his father to let him have the lessons at home. So the boxing coach comes to the Upper East Side every Sunday. Chris's father had a heavy bag and a speed bag installed in the basement, next to the unused stationary bicycle and treadmill. Still, Chris is not a particularly quick study. The big black gloves look like anvils sprouting from his skinny arms.

"Stay on your toes," Coach tells him.

Chris is tired and getting sloppy with his footwork, as he is shadowboxing, and his footwork is suspect to begin with. He is shining with sweat, and it has soaked semicircles into his designer tank top. Coach rolls his eyes every time he sees the skinny kid wearing the stupid-ass thing.

"All right, that's enough. Here." Coach hands him a leather jump rope. "This for ten minutes, and then you're done." Ten minutes is a long time. Coach settles himself in an overstuffed leather chair to wait for the kid to finish and go get the cash for the lesson.

Chris takes the rope and starts jumping, but trips when he hears the door buzzer, then stops jumping and goes to the intercom. "Who is it?"

"Sara."

"Oh . . . yeah, come in." Chris wonders if he looks good, with the boxing and everything.

Coach watches the girl walk in the room and notes what she looks like. Pretty, though Coach is not that impressed. The girl looks a little off. But he also suspects she might be a fighter in her own way.

Sara starts talking immediately. "Chris, guess what? Jessica says she can get some Twelve for the party."

"Hey! C'mon." Chris beckons her up the stairs with him as he drops the jump rope on the floor. "I'll be right back, Coach."

Out of earshot, on the second floor: "Are you nuts?"

"What?"

"You were just talking about that stuff in front of my coach."

"So what? Chill out, he just works for your dad or whatever, right? What's he gonna do? He probably doesn't even know what it is."

"I didn't even know you were into drugs."

"For the party, stupid."

Chris grabs four twenties for the hour of boxing out of his father's bureau. "I guess. But you shouldn't talk about it in front of him, okay?"

Sara says nothing, vaguely perturbed by Chris's lecture. Back downstairs, Chris hands over the money. Coach gets up and looks at the rope on the floor and then at Chris, who shrugs; Sara arches her eyebrows at the exchange. Coach cracks his knuckles, says, "See you next week."


Chris falls into the armchair Coach was sitting in. He is flexing his pecs, as if to make it seem they are always that big. Sara does not notice.

"Who do you think will come?" he asks.

"Maybe you." Sara exercises a grin onto her face for him. Chris practically giggles as he rises to try to catch her and kiss her. She fends him off.

"But seriously," he says, "I don't want to have too many people."

"Oh, why not?"

"You know how it gets. They might wreck the house or break something. Remember Paul's party?"

"Yeah. You told me you broke a coffee table."

"No, but something like that could happen if we have a lot of people."

Sara draws her chin back into her neck, like *Eew*.

"It could still just be you and me, alone, you know?" says Chris. "We're alone right now, actually . . ."

"No!" She barely holds in another *eew*. "I mean we have to have everybody cool so it will be the best party ever. A famous party, and we'll be, like, famous."

"I just don't want too many people."

"You want me, don't you?"

He nods his head. She moves closer and starts pushing into him, just walking into him as if he isn't there, pushing him back toward the chair. The backs of his legs hit it, and he sits down. He looks up at her face as she stands over him.

"Just leave the people to me, okay?" she says.

Chris is turning red.

Sara kisses his temple. "Great. Now just give me some cash to pay for your part of the stuff. Jessica said she had to take a lot of money out of her father's account, and I can't cover all of it."

Chris is not planning on doing any of the drug, but what the fuck, it's an investment. "Come upstairs, I'll grab the money. How much?"

"Two hundred. I'll stay here, though."

# 44

AFTER HE GIVES Sara the money ("See you tomorrow," no good-bye kiss), Chris goes upstairs to take a shower. As he passes his brother's room, he opens the door and sticks his head in. The shades are drawn, and it is dark. At the far end of the room, a single small lamp shines on the table Claude is sitting before. A white cloth is spread over the table and dark bits of metal lie across it, glistening with grease in the halo of light. Claude has grease on his hands. There is a small smear on his neck. He leans over his Uzi with a screwdriver, manipulating some tiny mechanism. His fingers work gently, with a great care that strikes Chris as not like Claude at all.

Chris remembers when he and Claude were both younger and their father gave them a model plane to build. It had an engine and could fly if put together correctly. About halfway through the project, Claude realized that he had made a mistake and the plane could never be completed. He grabbed the plane out of Chris's hands and smashed it against the wall. It scared the nanny, who tried to comfort Claude as she cleaned up the shattered bits of plastic and he cried, sobbing and screaming that "nothing ever works."

Chris cried too, at the loss of the plane. After Claude stormed off to his bedroom, the housekeeper held Chris in her arms until he cried himself out. The next day, Chris asked his mother for another plane. When he got it, one of the handymen assembled it so he could fly it off the roof of the town house. This is what Chris is remembering when he opens the door to Claude's room and sees that the television is on in the far corner, the only source of light besides the lamp. A tape of Claude's beloved professional wrestling plays muted.

"Hey, Claude."

Claude looks up quickly from the gun. The lamp casts yellow light on his features and reflects in and out of the beads of sweat on his forehead.

"I'm takin' a shower."

Claude decides he wants to take a shower too.

So the two brothers take showers in their separate bathrooms. Chris uses shampoo and conditioner and masturbates in the shower and then gets out and puts on his acne cream and brushes his hair forward and looks at himself shirtless in front of the mirror. Claude uses only shampoo in the shower. He turns the water as hot as he can take it, and then he turns it ice cold. He grips the shower-curtain bar each time he changes the temperature. And each time it is hotter and colder, and hotter and colder and hotter, until his skin is scalded red.

# 45

MOLLY IS WONDERING what to do about this guy Tobias. He called her again, asking her to come over and "chill" with him. She doesn't call him back. Instead, she calls her friend Mike and asks if she can come over.

"Of course." White Mike is glad she is coming over, but he has to switch modes.

White Mike and Molly have been friends since that Bahamas trip. And Molly was at the funeral for White Mike's mom, but she never saw White Mike cry. She saw Charlie cry about it, though, and White Mike's father. And Molly spent the night at White Mike's house once when her parents had one of their huge marathon fights. White Mike is always surprised by Molly's beauty and, for some reason, is glad they didn't go to the same school. He tidies the house before she arrives.

"How's working with your dad going?" Molly wants to know. "Glad you're taking the year off?"

"Yeah. It takes up all my time, but I'm learning a lot. I think I know how to run a restaurant."

"What do you do? Like, what's your day like?"

"I work late." He hates this. "But the nice thing is that I can sleep late, right, so I go in at around one, and then I'm, like, my dad's assistant. I do errands and bookkeeping and stuff like that, and then at night sometimes I'll be the host, or help out the waiters or be a bar bat or whatever. Then I help close up and get home at around three, and read for a while and then go to sleep."

"But you have Mondays off?"

"Not really, but Mondays and Tuesdays are the slowest," he says, not looking at her. "How about you? Still the smartest girl in school?"

"Think you're going to go to college next year?"

"That's not what you came over to talk about."

Molly throws her hair. He knows her so well.

"Well, there's this guy," she says. White Mike smiles as Molly laughs and shifts in her chair. "Yeah. He invited me to this big New Year's Eve party. As his date, I guess, I'm not even really sure."

White Mike runs through all the parties he knows are happening. "Where's the party?"

"Chris somebody and Sara Ludlow."

White Mike tries to keep his face straight. "What's the guy like?"

"He's actually a model. Tall, brown hair, kind of long. Really handsome."

"Well, what's the problem?" *I know the damn problem*, thinks White Mike. *The guy's a pothead. And an asshole.*

"Well, I don't know, I'm sort of suspicious of those parties, you know. And models are jerks."

"Yeah, I know."

"No, I'm serious, I don't know, he just doesn't seem like the kind of guy I'd like. I don't know."

"Well, those parties can get weird."

"Have you ever been to one?"

"Mostly they're not really even parties, just a bunch of kids getting wasted, listening to music, flirting with each other."

"I think I might go. You should come too."

"Maybe I'll stop by."

He tells Molly it is his father at the restaurant when his beeper goes off. *I am those parties,* thinks White Mike.

# 46

ANDREW HAS NOTHING to do. He walks with no destination in mind and ends up in Carl Schurz Park near Gracie Mansion where the mayor lives.

A tall man with a knitted wool cap pulled over his ears is sitting alone at a stone table with a chessboard painted on it. There is a little pom-pom on top of the cap, and his bristly white mustache glistens with moisture from his condensed breath. His pores are huge, craterous, even from the distance at which Andrew views him. There are chess pieces covering the board before him. Apparently he is playing against himself. Andrew stands and watches the game. The man sits deep in thought for several more minutes. Andrew pretends to study the board while he studies the man and his bulbous pink nose. Finally the man moves a pawn one space. He does so with startling force, a sharp bang as he whaps the piece down on the stone. He gets up, circles the table, and looks at the game from the inverse perspective.

Andrew walks a little closer to the table. The man still does not look up; just exhales heavily, sending a plume of white mist into the air. He pulls his overcoat about him and readjusts his yellow scarf.

"Want to play?" He looks up suddenly and catches Andrew's eyes.

"Sorry?"

"Do you want to play," the man repeats impatiently.

"Umm, I'm not very good."

"Don't say *umm*."

"What?"

"Don't say *umm*. Am I going to have to repeat everything with you?"

"I'm not sure if I want to play, actually. I think I might have somewhere to go." Andrew begins to leave.

"Oh, bullshit. Stay and play. It's your move."

Andrew looks at the old man incredulously but sits down.

"There we go."

"Don't you want to start a new game? I think I interrupted yours."

"Nonsense. Play what is there. You have the advantage. You'll need it."

Andrew looks hard at the board. He decides he really wants to beat the old man. They play in silence. The man slowly pushes Andrew into a corner. They both ignore the cold. When the man scores Andrew's queen, he takes out a long-stemmed oak pipe and a bag of tobacco and taps down a bowl. His match flares in the cold afternoon, and he lights the pipe and sucks on it silently, looking at the boy across from him as much as at the board. Three moves later he has the boy in checkmate.

"You played better than I thought you would."

"Thanks, I guess. I'm Andrew."

"Sven." They shake hands.

"What happened to your head?" He points at the bandage around Andrew's forehead.

"I got run over by an ice-skater."

Sven laughs a hacking old-man laugh around his pipe. "Fell down, did you? Ahh, heehee. Well then, what are you doing out here in the middle of the day, a youngster like you? Don't have any friends, huh? You a loser?"

"What? Whatever, man. Thanks for the game." Andrew starts to move away.

"Well now, wait up a moment. Come and I'll buy you a drink. Don't say *man*." Sven gets up and packs the pieces into a little plastic bag and puts it in a pocket of his old overcoat. He limps off a little ways, then turns back to Andrew, who is standing by the table. "Are you coming or not?"

"Umm, yeah, yeah." Andrew jogs over to catch up, as tall old mustachioed Sven limps off toward the edge of the park. "So where're we going?"

"You'll see when we get there."

"Hold up, I want to know where we're going."

"Well, Mr. Big Britches, if you're that uppity, we're going to O'Reilly's."

"Oh. Okay."

"You know the place, do you?" Sven grins. "Aren't you a little young to be drinking?"

"I pass by it all the time."

"Live around here?"

Uneasily: "Yeah."

"Ahh, don't worry, I'm not going to come and rape you."
Sven turns suddenly on the boy and shoves his face close—
"Boo!" Andrew starts, then lets out a sigh as Sven hoots with
laughter. "Be strong."

# 47

THERE WAS A bum whom White Mike walked by every day on the way home from grammar school. He was short, with light dark skin and bad acne and a long chin and a narrow nose and a big Afro that he wore with a sweatband sometimes, and he was always exercising—push-ups, sit-ups—on an exercise mat. He was rag-ass, but clean by White Mike's bum standards. His name, as far as White Mike knows, was Captain. That was how he introduced himself when White Mike handed him half a roast-beef sandwich one day. Lettuce, tomato, mustard, cheddar cheese, no mayonnaise, pickles.

Captain asked: "Where's the mayo?"

"Sorry," said White Mike.

"No, I mean not for me." He gave a great whooping laugh and turned the heads of the people waiting for the bus. "I mean you, you don't like mayo? Mayo's good, brotha."

"I never liked it much."

"I'm Captain, nice to meet you." The man extended his hand. White Mike felt how it was rough like sandpaper, callused and hard.

"Mike."

"Mike, huh? Well, you know, got to finish my workout." Captain went back to his mat and started exercising. Captain was the strongest guy White Mike knew. He did push-ups one-handed on his fingertips and crazy sit-ups and all sorts of stuff. White Mike could have done chin-ups on Captain's arm.

# 48

THE BAR IS empty. It is not even five o'clock. Sven leads An-drew to a table in the back. The bartender nods at him on the way in. As soon as they sit, a young waitress comes up. She is pretty, dark red hair and big brown eyes. She speaks with an Irish lilt. "Hi, Sven."

"Evening, Megan. Could I have a Dewar's and soda, please, and the same for the young man."

Megan smiles at them both with slightly crooked teeth and strides off to the bar. Sven removes his overcoat and gloves and hat to reveal faded vest with a pocket watch, and sun-splotched hands and a great mane of gray hair to match his bristly mustache. They sit in silence until she returns with the drinks. "Here you go. Cheers."

"Thank you, dear." Sven takes a drink and settles himself in his chair. "Now then. What is your story, Andrew?"

"My story?"

"More repeating, eh?"

"Well, what do you mean?" Andrew is already thinking about how he is going to tell the story of this bizarre afternoon to Sara, the hot girl from the hospital. *This crazy old dude Sven is sitting in the park alone, playing chess with himself. He gets me to play with him, and then he beats me, and then he takes me to O'Reilly's. Yeah, O'Reilly's. And he buys me a Scotch and soda.*

"Everybody has stories. Tell me a story. What do you do?"

"I'm a student." Andrew decides he does not like Scotch and soda.

"Of what?"

"I go to high school."

"What do you study?"

"Everything. You have to study everything. Remember? Didn't you go to high school?"

"Well, what is your passion? What do you want to be when you grow up?"

"A fireman. So I can drive the truck."

"Don't bullshit me."

"Why do you want to know?"

"Why don't you?"

Andrew can hardly keep himself from laughing. "I can't believe this. Okay. I think I'm interested in medicine."

"Well, then, a doctor." Sven finishes his drink and motions to Megan for another. "Got a strong stomach?"

"I guess."

"It is a bad thing to guess about if you want to be a doctor." Sven takes a swallow. "You need a strong stomach."

"What do you do?"

Sven looks at Andrew for a second and then back down into the bottom of his glass. He speaks slowly, motioning with his free hand and pronouncing every word. "I was in Japan once, on a fishing boat in the sea. It is beautiful there, a great expanse of blue, the sky over the ocean, and in the evening it all shimmers." His eyes focus elsewhere as he takes another sip. "This was years ago, and we went out in little skiffs to finish off the whales. We were whalers. I learned to speak Japanese. I threw the last harpoon, the coup de grâce, and it pierced the whale's lung." He suddenly pantomimes throwing a spear, and Andrew jumps and grips the table. "And then it flipped its tail up through the water as it was dying and knocked the boat over, and we were all in the water. And there was blood in the water from where the whale was bleeding and rolling, so sharks started to come. Now, the big boat was maybe three hundred yards off, and it started speeding over, but not before we were in a school of sharks. These blue-gray bodies swimming all about us. You would knock them in the nose with a piece of wood from the boat, but they kept coming. And some were ripping meat from the whale, and finally one got to me."

"So you're the old man and the sea," Andrew says, searching the man for scars or missing fingers.

Sven finishes his second drink. "Well, then. It came up behind me, and I could feel its teeth tear at my calf, and sure enough it ripped the muscle right off. The water all around felt warmer for the blood, I remember it perfectly. And then the boat got there and pulled us up out of the water. The other two from the boat were unharmed. But there was no doctor on the boat, so they took me in to shore to try and get my leg fixed up. I knew it was hopeless. The calf was just gone. Back on land they brought me to the man who was supposed to be the doctor. He was really just a gardener, and he would dispense herbs from his garden or grind them into potions for the village. But when he saw my leg, he had to run and be sick. I was lucky; there was an Englishman passing through on a tour of the country, and he was a much better doctor. He fixed me up. That is why you had better have a strong stomach if you want to be a good doctor. But then you never said you wanted to be a good doctor. You just said you were interested in medicine."

Andrew just stares at him.

"Well, then. Haven't you anything to say?"

"That's why you limp?"

"That is correct."

"That must be some scar on your leg."

Sven smiles and his face crinkles. He relishes the moment. "Want to see?" He brings his leg out to the side of the table and pulls up his corduroy pant leg. There is a metal prosthesis up to the knee.

"Oh. Sorry."

"So what classes do you take?"

Andrew decides to leave off the APs and honors from the names of his classes. "Molecular biology, English, calculus, European history, and Latin." He counts them off on his fingers.

"Latin. Not *Laddin*."

"Yeah, well, it's not my favorite class."

"Who are you reading? Caesar? '*Gallia est omnis divisa in partes tres . . .*'"

"No. Catullus."

"Ahh. I'm afraid I don't remember any."

Andrew glances at the old man's half-empty glass. "So what do you do now, Sven?"

"In Japan, the sands are black in places. Pitch black."
Andrew rolls his eyes, but Sven doesn't notice. "You could go
into the bazaars and buy or trade for anything. There were these
brightly colored fish and fruits and silk. And you could go to
some places and the girls would line up and you could choose
them and they would take you inside and make you tea or dance
and then for a couple dollars you could spend the night with
them. They were so small. Such tiny hands and feet." His eyes
are clouding again and his hands are trembling; he looks hungry
to Andrew. "Well, I don't need to tell you what that was like.
Been with a girl yet?"

Andrew takes out five dollar bills from his jeans and leaves
them on the table. "No. But I think I better be going."

"Where've you got to go? Sit down. You didn't even finish
your drink."

Andrew looks at the old man. "Sorry, Sven. I've got to go.
Nice talking to you, though. Maybe we'll play another game of
chess."

"Fine, then. Leave." Sven takes another swallow and re-
settles himself and looks at a painting on the wall. Andrew turns
and walks out, and Sven watches him go. "Watch out for the
old guy," Andrew says to Megan on the way out.

"Don't worry, love, I do."

# 49

WHITE MIKE IS beeped again right after Molly leaves. He knew it was coming. He has an ounce to sell to some kid up on Eighty-eighth Street and East End Avenue. He doesn't feel like going out this early, but it's a whole ounce, and shit, you know.

He takes a cab up there, does the deal, and decides to walk back down to another beep on Seventieth Street. As he is passing Seventy-seventh Street on York Avenue, he sees a construction site fenced off by yellow tape. There are no workers around, though. No tools, no trucks, nothing. In fact, there is nobody around.

White Mike walks into the site. There is tape tied to sharp iron poles surrounding a hole with a ladder going down into it. The hole is well lit and looks dry. White Mike finishes his examination of the hole and goes to continue on his way, but his backpack catches on one of the poles and rips. The bottom opens up, and the ounce of weed, in a plastic bag at the bottom of his backpack, falls out and slides into the hole.

"Shit." *How weird is this.*

White Mike looks around and, seeing no authority figures, ducks the tape and climbs down the ladder. A strong smell hits him as he descends, some mixture of sulfur and damp concrete. The hole is not as dry nor as bright as it looked from above. A couple feet away from the ladder on either side, in fact, it is dark enough so that White Mike is forced to bend down and search for the ounce with his fingers. There is steam coming from the walls, and it is humid like the streets in summer.

In the darkness, as he searches, a rat scurries away, bumping his foot. This scares him, but then he feels his heel on the Baggie and picks it up and climbs quickly back up the ladder.

# 50

CLAUDE IS IN his room, stripped to his underwear, practicing with the double-edged sword. He has taken it to a back corner of the room, where part of the wall is now chipped away and gouged. Claude spins and feints and then slashes out with the sword, and another chunk flies out of the wall. Claude examines his blade for nicks. Later, he sits on the edge of his bed with a whetstone, sharpening.

# 51

TWILIGHT IS DESCENDING, and White Mike is walking home through the clear cold air. He speeds up as he hears a screaming, a wailing. He can't make it out at first, this rasping howl. It is coming from around the corner in front of him. He hurries forward, and as he is passing the corner, the screaming is so loud he flinches. It sounds painful. He turns his head and he sees that it is Captain, and suddenly he can make out the words.

"I AM THE STRONGEST."

Captain is just at the edge of the building at the corner, and there is blood running off his hands where he has been dragging them along the stone wall. The snow underneath him is red and yellow from his blood and dog piss. Captain is not wearing a shirt, and his nipples stand distended from his huge chest. Every muscle in his stomach is perfectly defined. He jumps as he drags his arms, corded in fury, along the wall. He slams his head against the wall and slips as he lands. Blood comes down his face. White Mike is frightened, and the feeling is unfamiliar. Captain keeps screaming, writhing shirtless on the ground now in the piss-blood snow.

"I AM THE STRONGEST. I AM THE STRONGEST. I AM THE STRONGEST. I AM THE STRONGEST. I AM THE STRONGEST." He catches sight of Mike and rises, stumbling toward him. "I KNOW YOU. I AM STRONGEST. STRONGER. STRONGER. STRONGER."

White Mike dials 911 on his cell phone. People hurry past the screaming black man bleeding on the ground, trying not to see him. When the medics and police come and take the Captain, they thank White Mike and assure him that everything will be okay. They ask him if he's okay.

"Yeah, yeah, I'm fine."

# Part IV
# Monday, December 30

# 52

ANDREW SITS IN the kitchen and looks at the paper and eats crackers and drinks orange juice. He tells himself he is ready to call Sara Ludlow. He put it off all yesterday, but today he is going to call her. Just needs to get her number. Andrew figures the other kid, Sean, her boyfriend or whatever, is probably out of the hospital by now, so he will call him and get the girl's number and call her like he is just calling to get his CD back.

A West Indian accent answers the phone and tells Andrew that the young master is asleep.

Andrew switches rooms and drops himself on the couch with the remote. He channel-surfs for a couple hours, switching between the networks and their sitcoms and Comedy Central and MTV and VH1, on which he watches the Hundred Greatest Artists of Rock and Roll. Where's Sublime? When the countdown is finished, he calls again and this time gets Sean.

Andrew looks at the number he has written down. Now he has to call the girl. It is absurd for him to feel nervous. He sits down and looks at the paper again and has another glass of orange juice and some more crackers.

"Fuck it," he says out loud as he grabs for the phone and punches in her number.

"Hello?"

"Sara?"

"Yes?"

"This is Andrew, from the hospital, remember, you borrowed—"

"Oh, that's right. I love the CD. It's great. I've been listening to it, like, nonstop since I took it from you."

"Good."

"So you probably want it back, right?"

"Actually, not really."

"Well, let me burn it first. I have a friend with a burner who's having a New Year's party, actually. You should come."

Andrew smiles into the phone. "Yeah, definitely. Where is it?"

"Two East Ninetieth Street. Just off of Fifth. It's this kid named Chris, do you know him?"

"Probably. You sure it's okay if I just come?"

"Yeah, and bring people. It's an open house, and he wants a big party."

"So I'll see you there?"

"Yeah, I'll be there. Oh, you smoke?"

"Umm, yeah, sometimes." Twice, because they said the first time he wouldn't get high. Twice to see what it was like.

"Have you got any weed now?"

"Oh, yeah, sure."

"Okay, well, don't forget to bring it."

"No problem."

"Great. See you then. Bye."

Shit. Andrew doesn't have any weed. How is he gonna buy weed. Ask Hunter. Hunter's still in jail. Shit. Andrew tries to remember what those two little potheads in his school used to tell him. About how they had the hookup. Fifty ought to be enough.

# 53

TIMMY AND MARK Rothko are walking east on Eighty-sixth Street, two more white kids playing black. Fucking crazy. They are both wearing FUBU (For Us By Us) with their Timberland boots, sizes nine and ten respectively. Timmy is the brains of the operation, as it were. Mark Rothko is the muscle. Timmy is tremendously fat. He has man boobies, but they are concealed under his wife beater and all of his designer clothing. Mark Rothko dresses the same way.

Mark Rothko is called Mark Rothko because at his first school, on a trip to the Metropolitan Museum of Art, he shoved another kid into the real Mark Rothko's *Untitled* (*Number 12*). The huge painting came down on the kid, and both he and the painting had to be restored. And some other wiseass on the field trip started calling Mark Rothko as Mark Rothko and it stuck. Mark Rothko was kicked out of that school. Then a couple of other schools. He has no idea who the real Mark Rothko was ("some painter dude"), but he likes the name. Timmy knows him by no other.

Tonight the two of them are on a mission to score some weed. So Timmy whips out his celly to beep White Mike; Mark Rothko whips out his and starts to play Snake.

"Yo b, we gonna smoke some mad bowls tonight," Timmy says to Mark Rothko.

"Word, word," Mark Rothko agrees sagely.

"Yeah, and then we gonna find some hos. . . ." Timmy starts tapping some hypothetical ass and grinds his hips in the air. His center of gravity is low to the ground.

"Damn."

"Wassup?" Timmy looks up from his woman.

"You wanna go inside? It's mad cold out here."

"A'ight."

Timmy and Mark Rothko walk into HMV and head for the hip-hop section. They are short enough so the cashiers can't see them over the aisles as they stuff CDs into their cargo pockets. Mark Rothko breaks off for a minute and grabs James Taylor's greatest hits while Timmy isn't looking. He has heard his father listen to it. He gets back upstairs and finds Timmy doing his obscene dance in front of a poster of Jennifer Lopez. J. Lo is dressed like an Amazon warrior, complete with brass brassiere. Mark Rothko taps Timmy on the shoulder and they head for the door, all very smooth, and out before they break into a run. The store's siren wails behind them. They make it around the block and into Starbucks, where they order hot chocolate, huffing and puffing.

"Man, I gotta quit smokin'," mumbles Rothko.

"What?" Timmy gasps. "That's wack, man. Let's biggity bust."

Timmy and Mark Rothko take their hot chocolate and continue down the street to Mimi's Pizza, where Mark Rothko buys a broccoli slice with extra cheese.

"That shit's nasty, man," Timmy says.

Mark Rothko shrugs him off. Timmy drops into a chair and checks his celly. The Serbian guys behind the counter eye them.

"Yo, Rothko, we missed the call."

"Word? Dawg, call him back. I gots to get blizzy."

# 54

WHITE MIKE IS talking on the phone to a friend he went to school with, when he went to school. Warren, who goes to Harvard. He was White Mike's other best friend in high school. It was always Mike and Hunter and Warren.

"So how's the city?"

"The same, you know."

"Merry Christmas, by the way."

"Yeah, you too."

"How was it?"

"The same. My dad gave me cash. I never see him, you know, but he got a little tree for the kitchen table. He's sort of sentimental."

"Yeah, we got a big Christmas tree."

"When do you go back?"

"Monday, after New Year's. What are you doing for that?"

"Probably just make the rounds. There'll be a lot of calls. You?"

"Cancún with the whole family. Leave tonight."

"How'll that be?"

"Boring. I'm almost looking forward to going back to school."

"Yeah?"

"No, seriously. It's better up there than you think. You should come."

"Maybe."

"Yeah, right."

"Hey, man, I've been reading and everything. I still think like a student, sort of, you know?"

"There's no discipline."

"Discipline. My whole life is discipline."

"And so real."

"As if you were ever going to do anything but go to Harvard."

"Yeah. Well—"

"And you come back here like you're learning something important. I was walking along the street yesterday, going to sell my last ounce to that Alport kid, and my bag got caught on a pole and ripped, and the weed fell down into a hole."

"Okay."

"So I went down into the hole—it was a whole ounce—and it's all dark and humid down there, and there was a rat. And you know where I was?

"Hell? With Dante?"

"And you go to Harvard, and who do you think is learning more?"

"Don't be melodramatic." Warren flinches as White Mike whacks the receiver against the table.

"Hello? Mike?"

"I'm going to Coney Island."

# 55

AFTER SEAN GIVES Andrew Sara's cell-phone number, he tries to go back to sleep but can't because his arm hurts. And he wonders about Sara and this guy Andrew. And Sara and everyone else she flirts with, which seems to be everybody, depending on what she wants. He wonders if he cares, particularly.

He has to go back to the doctor in a couple of hours because the doctor wants to change his dressing and see how he is doing. So he gets up and goes through the difficult routine of dressing with a cast the size and shape, he thinks, of a crooked elephant penis. It is nothing like an elephant penis. His mother cut the sleeve off a sweatshirt, so he wears that. The housekeeper asks him if he would like some breakfast and he says sure, how about some French toast. She makes it, but he doesn't eat it. He never eats breakfast, and wonders why she hasn't figured that out. She tries to chat about his arm, and he takes a few bites so he doesn't have to talk. In the elevator on the way down to the lobby, he pushes the button marked TAXI. When he gets downstairs, one of the doormen has hailed a cab. Sean gets in.

The cabbie is a short white guy with a huge gut pushing up against the steering wheel. The interior smells artificially of air freshener and chocolate, as if he were inside one of the bags he used to carry his Halloween candy in. The reason, he sees, is that in the front seat is a big tub of candy. Tootsie Rolls, lollipops, bags of M&M's, bite-sized 3 Musketeers.

The license proclaims the driver Theodore Rimby, who smiles a big gap-toothed grin and wears a bow tie in his picture. He has a thick mustache and dimples. He wears a bow tie now, and a big Russian muff. It is cold in the cab; the heat is not on.

Sean gives Theodore the address and sits back.

"No problem. Goin' to see a doctor, huh? For your arm, maybe? I couldn't help noticing, but that's a heck of a cast you got there."

"Yeah." Sean is unimpressed by the cabdriver's deduction. The address, after all, was for Lenox Hill Hospital.

"I was in a hospital a little while ago. I had a heart attack, and boy, it was scary. But I got back into the cab fast, you know, gotta get back." Theodore jams a fat fist in the tub of candy. "Want something? I got a lot up here."

"No thanks."

"It's all wrapped already, if you're worried, don't worry."

"No thanks."

"Well, that's okay. I was a finicky eater too"—Sean narrows his eyes at the characterization—"of course, that all changed when I got a little bit older." Theodore laughs a big wheezy laugh, like a bus kneeling to let a wheelchair passenger get on. "Yeah, I've always loved candy, though, and I suppose everyone else does too. That's why I keep it in the cab. It's good for starting conversation."

Sean sits in silence. Then, vaguely annoyed, he says, "I don't really want to talk."

Unflustered, Theodore moves on. "Well, that's okay too. I know everyone says that cabdrivers ought to stay quiet, and that, you know, you won't get good tips if you talk all the time, but usually people tip just the same unless you say something that pisses 'em off real good or something like that. Most people want to talk. Don't have enough people to talk to. People tell me all sorts of things. Some still get pissed, though. This one guy, I was tellin' him some of what I was thinkin' about women at the time—you know the three C's of womanhood?"

Sean doesn't say anything.

"Cookin', cleanin', and childbearin'!" More laughter, like a heavy piece of machinery starting up. "Of course, if my wife ever heard me talking like that, she'd throw a shit fit, you know, but it's the truth."

In the backseat, Sean thinks of Sara and the hospital, and how she would look swollen with some baby, her breasts huge and heavier than they already are, gathered around her neck, all puffy and immobile with the extra weight, her hips gone from the pleasantly boyish supermodel size they are now to some other thing closer to what pretty women look like in old pictures. Like Marilyn Monroe, whom Sean has never found particularly attractive. Certainly not more attractive than any *Sports Illustrated* swimsuit model he has ever seen.

"You got a wife?"

Sean can think of nothing to say. "No."

"A girl?"

"Yeah."

"Never get married. It's not worth it. Guess I'm riskin' my

tip, all this jibber-jabberin'. Ahh, well. You don't want to talk, and we're nearly there."

Sean looks in the rearview mirror and sees Theodore's tired eyes, and the big tub of candy next to him that he is reaching into.

"Well, why'd you get married?"

"Oh," says Theodore, surprised, "well, they trick you, you know. And you love 'em. Or I loved mine."

"Loved?"

"Yeah, she passed away a couple of months ago, God rest her soul. I sure was glad to see the girls, though. They came back for the funeral. One of 'em, Emily, she's pregnant, can you believe it? I'm gonna be a grandfather. I'm trying to get her to come back for a visit, you know, but everyone is so busy. She lives in St. Louis. She says I shouldn't be a cabbie anymore, but I like it. It's honest work. I think that movie *Taxi Driver* spooked people. That Robert De Niro, he's really good. But crazy, huh? That's not what it's really like. You ever seen the movie?"

"No."

"Don't bother. That'll be five-thirty."

# 56

WHITE MIKE GETS on the F train at Fifty-first Street, and all but one seat is taken. He is going downtown, all the way to Coney Island, just to get out. He'll deal with the beeps later. It's still early. White Mike sits in the empty seat, pulling his overcoat tight around his shoulders and making himself small so he fits between the other passengers. At the next stop an old lady with white hair and a blue coat gets on the train carrying a bag and clings to the pole in the middle of the car in front of White Mike.

He has encountered this problem before. He can never decide whether to abdicate his seat to old ladies. What are old ladies doing on the train by themselves, anyway? Old ladies shouldn't have to ride the train by themselves. White Mike sighs and stands up and indicates to the old lady with a cough and a wave of his hand that the seat is hers. She doesn't get it, though he sees the other passengers notice. He taps the old woman on the shoulder and points to the seat, and she nods and smiles and sits down, dragging her bag between her legs. White Mike moves to the next car down and leans on the doors.

Coney Island is the last stop. A whole hour from where he got on, it is like another country, White Mike thinks, as he leaves the train. The place is all washed out in the gray of winter, and the cold bites even through his overcoat. White Mike walks with his head up because he is looking at the skeletal roller coasters and faded billboards. The place is practically deserted, and White Mike thinks it would be a good place to get kidnapped. It feels like an old part of New York. White Mike read *Ragtime* and liked the description of the decadence and the beach and the children playing and walking the boardwalk. He even recommended the book to Molly. No children now, though, only White Mike and what he perceives to be a transvestite hooker, although he isn't sure. He has seen hookers before, but he doesn't think he has ever seen one so tall or broad. White Mike keeps walking until he comes to the arcade on the boardwalk. He can hear the chirping electronics of virtual explosions and the roll of Skee-Balls over their wooden tracks. He walks in.

In a dark corner, there is a larger game with a big sensor pad in front of it that a short Latino kid in a tank top and parachute pants is standing on. His parka lies on the floor off to the side. The game is called Dance Dance Revolution, and White Mike watches as it counts down from three and starts. It plays music, a really fast techno samba with a driving beat, and arrows scroll up the screen. The kid on the pad is moving his feet where the arrows point, on beat with the music. The song is too fast, though, and he is missing the beats or stepping in the wrong direction; every time he screws up, the game beeps and the kid starts laughing. But his friends aren't laughing, and soon the kid stops. White Mike is watching discreetly a little ways away. The kid on the pad gets off, throwing his arms up at the fast music. He grabs his jacket and steps to the side. Pretty soon his turn runs out, and the machine requests another seventy-five cents. A taller black kid in a dark knit hat stands on the pad and puts in the money. He takes off his jacket and drops it on the floor. The kid is big, and his black sweatshirt is stretched a little over his shoulders. He looks strong. There is a cross hanging around his neck on a gold chain, and White Mike can't tell whether the stones on the cross are real, but he bets they are not.

The music comes on again, and the beat is even faster than before. The kid starts moving his feet, and it doesn't look anything like dancing. But the rhythm starts speeding up, and he isn't missing any of the beats and the machine hasn't beeped once, and his chain is swinging and bouncing off his chest. His arms are loose at his sides, and they swing as he moves his legs and hips. The music is getting faster, and the arrows are pointing in all different directions, and he's keeping up perfectly. White Mike sees the kid's face as he spins, and his eyes are closed. And still the machine hasn't beeped. The kid looks like he is in a trance, and his feet fly out from under him in all directions, and White Mike realizes, as the music speeds up even more, that of course the kid must have the patterns memorized. Then the kid plants a hand on the pad in place of a foot, and as the music speeds up even faster, he is dancing on his hands and feet, doing cartwheels and handstands in place to keep up. And it looks like break dancing, only White Mike cannot believe how graceful it is, and when he glimpses the kid's face again, it is completely relaxed, with the eyes closed easy, not shut tight, as in sleep.

The other kids aren't surprised by this, just watch intently and don't speak. After another minute of this silent frenzy of movement, the music finally stops, and the kid stands still as it ends and, after a moment, gets off the pad and picks up his jacket, and White Mike gets the feeling that the kid looked him right in the eye.

White Mike leaves the arcade, and something about how quiet the kids were, watching, reminds him of the two times he went to church with his mother. Both times were on Christmas Eve. White Mike didn't mind so much, though Charlie, who was with them, hated it. White Mike's mother loved Charlie, always had a particular place in her heart for him. Charlie always thought church was boring, and worse, that it delayed Christmas-present opening, but he went at the behest of White Mike's mother. She was the only one who could ever really make him do anything. White Mike never tried to tell Charlie that he actually liked going to the church, liked the wooden seats and the sense of ritual and order that came with sitting and half listening to the service.

White Mike is walking from the arcade over the sand down to the water. He does not stop for one of Nathan's world-famous hot dogs. Out of the corner of his eye, he sees a dealer talking to a white man with stringy hair. White Mike doesn't know how he knows the guy is a dealer, but he is sure of it. White Mike decides when he sees the drug dealer that this really is a seedy neighborhood and he doesn't feel like hanging around anymore. He looks out over the gray water for another minute; while the waves break and foam on the shore, he notes that the farther out he looks, the calmer it gets, until it is just a solid gray line. The horizon doesn't move.

*Just to make sure,* thinks White Mike, as he looks over the ocean, pointing his arms out in front of him. He thinks: *England.* Than he points left: *Canada.* Right: *Mexico.* He turns around and points again: *California. Just to make sure,* he thinks.

# 57

WHITE MIKE GETS off the train back uptown and is beeped by his most amusing customers. The *thuglings,* White Mike calls them in his head. Timmy and Mark Rothko. They have missed his call to set a place. So he figures he'll make the little fuckers walk. Instead of calling, he sends a text message for them to meet him at Forty-fifth and Fifth in an hour. White Mike wants to walk down Fifth Avenue. He likes looking at all the pretty girls as they pass by. Fifth Avenue is a river of them. White Mike feels like he looks good himself. Sometimes he catches girls staring at him from a distance, and he thinks they do this because he looks a little like a movie star with the overcoat and the jeans. He walks with a purpose, he has somewhere to go. *I have something to do,* he thinks, and that is important, and it makes him walk a better way, and it clears the afternoon.

# 58

"FUCKIN' FORTY-FIFTH Street? What in the damn shiz fo a niz?"

# 59

WHEN WHITE MIKE was fifteen, he had acne on his face that he squeezed because he thought it cleansed his soul. He actually felt cleaner when he did not have the dirt-headed worms burrowed into his fair skin. He was handsome, and he knew it. But he also knew that he wouldn't be attractive, really, with the acne.

His mother picked up on his distress and made him an appointment with her dermatologist. She made it seem like he had no choice, because she knew he would never go on his own, that he would think he was going in for cosmetic treatment. So she told him he had to go get the warts burned off his knee, and why not ask the doctor what she thought about the acne.

So White Mike walked up Fifth Avenue to the dermatologist's office. White Mike always liked Fifth Avenue. It was fall and the leaves were turning, and as they piled, the doormen dressed like midranking Soviet officers swept them into the gutter. White Mike supposed all the doormen looked exactly the same by design. You saw only the uniform. And so many. White Mike was counting things as he walked. Five blocks, four West Indian women pushing strollers (*he recognized the dialect because there were so many West Indian nannies:* shit n'man, *he could imitate,* who de ass gonna say dat ta me?), *two kids in polo shirts on skateboards, one motorcycle, twenty-one doormen so far. It seemed to White Mike that there were always more doormen guarding the bright buildings and ready to help than there were people coming out of them who needed either protection or help.*

*One doorman took out his whistle and walked into the street, blowing it, trying to hail a cab. A woman in all black and simple gold jewelry looked expensive as she waited under the awning; and then gracefully, because she had much practice, though it is hard to do gracefully, she got into the cab in one fluid motion as the doorman held the car door and then closed it behind her.*

*There was a woman with a cat on a leash, a gray and white animal, walking down Fifth Avenue. White Mike didn't stare at the cat, but he noticed as it stepped over the little wrought-iron fence around a tree and clawed at the bark. The woman waited patiently, holding the leash. She was wearing a fur coat that came up to her square double chin. Her hair was frizzy and gray and flew out, straight back behind her head. As White Mike walked by, he thought:* I'll never be old.

# 60

WHITE MIKE IS just passing FAO Schwarz and can see huge animals in the window, bigger than he, some of them as big as a small car. Lions and tigers and bears as big as Hondas. White Mike, with the cool air clearing his head on Fifth Avenue, thinks this is funny and, on a whim, walks into the toy store.

It is frenzied inside, even right after Christmas. There are tourists everywhere. White Mike walks to the bear area. There is a big pile of the stuffed creatures on the floor, and kids are climbing all over them. He picks up one of the animals. It is soft and warm and well made, a medium-size polar bear on sale for $99. White Mike strokes it and puts it back down. Then, off to the side, he sees one little boy with curly blond hair clasping a bigger bear's head in his arms. The boy is looking right at White Mike and is chewing on the bear's ear. He is chewing the bear's ear off. White Mike turns his gaze and leaves the store quickly.

# 61

MARK ROTHKO WENT *downtown one night, with Timmy, to buy a fake ID. Timmy knew this place on Bleecker Street that had a sign advertising* ID PICTURES, *and he had gotten his ID there. The place was fluorescent-lit and dingy but well stocked with magazines and candy and cigarettes and a copy machine. The man behind the counter showed them a card minus the picture. It had a repeating hologram of the Ohio state flag, the buckeye. He said to Mark Rothko: "Never fails. Only forty dollars."*

*"Yeah, let's do this."*

*The man pulled his long hair back in a ponytail. Timmy looked at him. The man directed Mark Rothko to stand in front of a white screen, and with a digital camera, he lined up the shot. Then he lowered the tripod and lined up again and finally took the picture. Mark Rothko was awed by the myriad of possibilities opening like a flower in his mind as he held the card and looked into his own eyes. He had a new date of birth. He was born again.*

# 62

JESSICA WAKES IN her room, surrounded by her teddy-bear collection. Big bears from FAO Schwarz, little soft bears, old bears with button eyes, brown bears, black bears, all sprawled with her on the bed. The first thing she thinks of is the Twelve she is going to score the next day. *What a drug,* she thinks. *That is a drug for people like me. Tonight, tonight, tonight.* That guy Lionel will come to the party and she'll give him the money and she'll get high. She's got only about three hundred dollars left, but she'll get some other kids to chip in for the sake of the party, and it will all work out.

Jessica doesn't have anything to do until later, when she has to go out to lunch with her mother, so she stays in bed and turns on the TV so she can watch the late-morning talk shows. Jerry Springer and the dregs of humanity, engaged in their backstabbing incestuous homosexual bisexual overweight gothic bizzaro wet-hot fucking and stealing and lying. Jessica is, like, disgusted, you know, but, like, weirdly fascinated also. Maybe that's why sometimes she inquires about the maid's son, who is in trouble all the time. *Bitch,* she thinks of herself. Maybe she deserves to die, she thinks. Maybe someone ought to kill her. *Pop.* Easy. Shot in the head and then everyone bullshits a eulogy and the parents cry, right, because she was such a lovely girl, such a wonderful, wonderful girl. *Pop pop,* someone comes into school and pulls the trigger. And then they're on television and Jessica lies bleeding and people sit transfixed in front of the television watching it all unfold on CNN and the police come and tie it all up in yellow crime-scene ribbon and send it to you as a gift to unwrap and fuck with and get off on. Right? So someone could just pop her. *Pop.* And she's dead and then everyone would do some more thinking and she'd be dead and would never get to *eew* again, never get to be a bad wife and then a bad parent. Just *pop. Gonna fucking kill that bitch first.* Jessica dazedly arranges her stuffed animals in a circle and talks to them, listens as she hears them talk to one another. It's like the best talk show ever.

"Yeah, point the camera here, we'll have a talk show, sit there," says Jessica. "So there is a lot of fucked-up stuff in our school, isn't there?"

"Yep," says little brown Teddy with the black button eyes.

"They all have bad taste in music, they're all assholes," says Betty, the big soft pink bunny.

"Right. Makes you just want to kill the fuckin' bitch," says Teddy.

"Ha ha, that's right, but we're not serious. We're not crazy, but who would you kill first and how, if you were to kill someone there?" asks Betty the bunny.

"Well, I think I'd have to kill that Jessica bitch first," says Teddy. "You know I'd take the gun and be like *pop pop.* Right in the back of the head. Make her kneel like she does for the blow jobs she gives to all those football assholes." Teddy turns his button eyes to Jessica. "And then, if you were looking at the front of her face, it would seem to bulge out for just a split second, and then there would be blood all in front of her, and she would fall into it and hit her nose, and maybe break it because it might have been weak from surgery or something. And then CNN would come in and get the shot, and then schools across the country could have a moment of silence for the horrible, inexplicable massacre.

"Could we have a moment of silence, please," continues Teddy, now solemnly, "for those who died. And now could we please have a moment of silence for those who killed them."

# 63

ON THEIR WAY downtown, Timmy and Mark Rothko stop in the Star Deli to buy cigarettes. The deli is clean and well lit but empty right now. The dark-skinned man behind the counter eyes them as they move quickly to the back of the store. Buying cigarettes requires more poise and human contact than shoplifting CDs. Finally, they shuffle up to the counter and look up at the packs of cigarettes behind the man. He looks down his nose at them, and Mark Rothko shifts uncomfortably in his big frame. He is still nervous about stuff like this from the time a guy snapped his fake ID in two. On the counter is a calendar that has the date on which you must be born to purchase cigarettes. Mark Rothko tries not to look at it and says: "Pack of Parliaments."

"You got ID?"

Mark Rothko rolls his eyes in disgust and searches for his wallet in his cavernous cargo pockets. Timmy fiddles with the candy. Mark Rothko finds his wallet and takes out the Ohio ID card. In the picture, his head is tilted down toward the camera in an effort to throw shadow on his chin. Short in a head shot.

The man looks at the ID card, snorts at Mark Rothko, and drops it on the counter. "No, is fake."

"No? What the fuck, motherfucker? Don't hate the playa, hate the game!"

Timmy likes the sound of that and jumps in himself. "Yeah, what de dilly, you damn camel jockey? He's eighteen, give 'im the cigarettes. See the ID?"

"Is fake."

"Is not fake, motherfucker."

"Leave or I call the police." The man reaches toward the phone.

"How 'bout I call my foot up yo ass." Mark Rothko feints his double chin at the man. Timmy waves his hand sideways in imitation of gangsta music videos and concurs: "Word. Tell 'im. S'all breezy on the heezy fo sheezy mah neezy."

The man looks at Timmy and then leans across the counter and stares at Mark Rothko, right in his little blue eyes. "I have this," he says, pulling a revolver, old and battered, from beneath the counter and holding it over his head.

Timmy and Mark Rothko bolt for the door, Timmy shouting, "Shit, he busted out the nine milly and gonna pop a cap in yo cracka ass!"

The shopkeeper is surprised at how fast the boy said all that. He puts the empty handgun back under the counter.

# 64

IN THE WAITING *room at the dermatologist's office, there were old women with faces that made White Mike suddenly understand why the Indians called white people pale demons. The women's eyes were open a little too wide, or slit just a little too narrow, all the time. One of them with a tiny chin was flapping ostrichlike at the terrified girl behind the desk.*

*"It's very disrespectful. I've been waiting here for an hour, and I have another appointment that I simply must go to now."*

*"I'm very sorry—"*

*"And I simply can't do this, I have an appointment to keep, and now I have to reschedule in a week or two weeks or a month or three months."*

*"We have an opening next Monday. Any time up to nine o'clock in the morning."*

*"What about nine-fifteen?"*

*One of the other girls behind the counter shook her head, and the woman saw it and shot her a look.*

*   *   *

*In the examination room, a Chinese woman popped the black-heads out of White Mike's face with a silver tool, and he stared at her eyes and his reflection in the magnifier attached to her head like a miner's lamp.* This is a woman whose job it is to pop pimples, *thought White Mike.*

*White Mike thought about jobs and what color his eyes were. He could see his eyes in the reflection, and they were blue. Light blue eyes, thought White Mike. Not blue fire, not ice, not the sky, not the sea, just blue. And it pissed White Mike off. He thought about his father's job.* He gives people a place to eat. This woman pops pimples. *His mother who sent him to this woman to pop pimples and used to teach people about anthropology, the study of man. White Mike wondered, of course, what his job would be. Maybe he would pop pimples for a living.*

# 65

JESSICA IS HAVING lunch with her mom at some bistro on Madison Avenue. It is a place of bisques and pâtés and teas and sorbet. Jessica is unsure why her mother wants to have lunch. It is not something they do. They are not best friends. They order small salads, Diet Cokes, one linguini with clam sauce, and one grilled monkfish.

"So how are you, Jessica?"

"Fine, you know"—she laughs a little laugh nervously, this is weird—"the same."

"Your report card came."

Jessica doesn't say anything. Her grades dropped last quarter from A's to B's. She knows why: she didn't do the work. She was busy.

"Yeah?"

"Well, Jessica, I know you try really hard, but with college applications coming up and everything, I thought we could maybe . . . rethink things."

"What do you mean, like a new tutor or something?"

"Well, no. I was wondering though, is something wrong? Is something upsetting you?"

"No."

"Because I was thinking if something was, upsetting you that is, then you might want to go and see this doctor I know."

"A shrink?"

"Well, yes, I suppose, but you know, I go to one. Lots of people do."

"A lot of girls at school go to one."

"Yes, see, and I thought that maybe you might want to talk to somebody who wasn't so close, you know, and that might help you get your grades up. Because you know your father has his heart set on you going to at least Wesleyan."

"Whatever, Mommy. I don't need a shrink."

"It might make you feel better. It always helps me. It's just talking to someone to help you see things more clearly."

"I don't know what I would talk about."

"Oh, you'd find things to talk about. Look at your grades. There must be something."

"Okay, whatever. I'll go. Just tell me when."

"You'll be happy you went."

At school, Jessica knows girls who talk about how they try to fuck with their shrinks. Or how they actually try to fuck their shrinks. How they lie to them and make things up about their lives. One girl who is a terrible student talks about how she could ace her classes but is frustrated by the stupid teachers who don't even make it hard enough to be interesting. She says she isn't challenged. The ugly girl who never has boyfriends complains about boy troubles. Jessica starts thinking of things she'll talk about. Not Twelve.

# 66

"WHAT DE DILL, Mike?" inquires Timmy as they roll up to meet White Mike on the corner of Forty-fifth and Fifth.

"Don't talk that shit to me." They start walking. "Fifty?"

"Yeah, fiddy," says Timmy.

"Fiddy," say Mark Rothko, chuckling. White Mike just looks at him. Mark Rothko gets nervous and turns away. He nudges Timmy, who removes a crumpled fifty-dollar bill from his pocket and palms it to White Mike while he hands Timmy a plastic film canister full of weed and turns away from them, downtown.

Mark Rothko is suddenly so happy he bursts into quiet song and busts out the pimp walk. "S'all about the Benjamins, baaabyyy . . ."

As White Mike is walking away, Timmy calls out to him. "Yo, Mike, hold up, I got a custie for you."

White Mike waits with his back to them as they catch up.

"He went to my school. His name is Andrew. Called me for the hookup, 'cause he knows I got the connection. Can he get some?"

"It's on you if he's a fuck-up, Timmy."

"Yeah, no problem. He'll probably beep you tonight. Here's his number." Timmy hands White Mike a Broadway show stub. Timmy had grabbed it from beside his mother's phone. *The Producers.*

"Peace, White Mike," says Timmy

"Right." And White Mike walks away.

Timmy and Mark Rothko head to Timmy's roof to smoke a fatty jay.

# 67

IN CENTRAL PARK *the fall that White Mike didn't go to college, there was a gang of skater kids who hung around by the little half-dome amphitheater near Seventy-second Street. They spent the afternoons smoking and doing tricks while old men played chess around them and the fit people Rollerbladed and jogged past and dogs got walked. White Mike first saw the skaters by chance but then kept coming back. He waited for his beeps on the benches and watched the skaters. It was pleasant. The weather was good.*

*The skaters would stack their boards sideways, and then someone would try to ollie over them. Some of the kids were pretty good. They could clear three boards. A lot of air. The tallest kid, one of the best skaters, always had a cigarette in his hand while he skated, and as he would glide by, sometimes he would take a long, elegant drag and the smoke would float behind him. He would hold the cigarette even as he did tricks, and after he landed a trick, he would take another drag. He wore big bag-ass pants and skate shoes and wraparound reflective Oakley sunglasses and a backward Yankees baseball cap. He never fell. The first time White Mike saw him, he cleared four boards, arms out to the side like some bird of prey, with the cigarette smoking at the end of one long arm, and landed on the other side smooth and easy. White Mike was impressed.*

*White Mike did not start skateboarding, but he thought that even if he didn't get that out of seeing the skaters, he got the place out of it. And that dome and stage became one of his favorite places in the city, and he went there all the time, even at night. He knew that it was twenty of his strides across the stage, and that when he walked those steps, his overcoat billowed to the outside because the dome caught the wind and turned it around.*

# 68

JAIL ISN'T AS bad as Hunter thought it was going to be. For one thing, he had ID on him, so he spent more than the first day in the local precinct holding cell and didn't have to go downtown till later. And it wasn't so bad even down there. No one really paid any attention to him. In fact, he was struck by the carelessness from cops and criminals alike. He guessed it was a slow day. He did a lot of thinking while he was in the cell, because he figured push-ups were clichéd and he didn't want to look like a fool. He tried to remember all the things he had ever memorized for school, but all he could really call up was the beginning of the *Aeneid* in Latin, *Arma virumque cano, I sing of arms and the man.* He thought that was appropriate.

Not that he wasn't scared sometimes. But Hunter knew he hadn't killed anybody, and knowing you're innocent is a strong thing in an enclosed space.

Hunter is thinking how much he'd like to talk to someone. White Mike would be best, but almost anybody would do. Or maybe not. Maybe he never wants to talk to anybody again, ever.

At some point in the afternoon, an officer shows up and takes him to another room where a lawyer he has never met before introduces himself. The lawyer has Hunter's father on the phone.

"So I guess Andrew's father found you?"

"Yes, Hunter, he's been very helpful, and it was so good of him to track us down. We left you our itinerary, you know."

"I know."

Silence.

"Yes. In any case, I'll be flying out first thing in the morning, as I said. It's the best I can do. Jesus, who could ever expect anything like this."

"I know."

"I'm sorry this is all taking so long."

There is another pause on the phone. *He's the dad, let him figure it out*, thinks Hunter. *Let him know what to say next.*

"How are you feeling?"

Hunter shakes his head and closes his eyes.

"Pretty shitty, Dad."

# 69

MATT MCCULLOCH HANGS up the phone, exhausted. His wife was already asleep with her pills before he even made the call. He made sure of that, didn't want to have to listen to her. He mixes another gin and tonic and looks out to the beach. He supposes his son is scared.

He remembers what happened to him when he was Hunter's age, and how scared he was then. He had been drinking heavily then too, but he remembers the whole thing. He was a junior in high school, boarding school for him. Also in the winter, but just before the holiday break. The parents would come up and see the boys sing a concert before the end of the term. They would sing carols and church songs. "Hallelujah Amen" as arranged by Handel, and things like that. And in his first two years, when he was really happy to be getting out of school, he would be up there singing and it would all click and hallelujahs would be raining down in song and filling the big auditorium, and he would get into singing, it made him feel good, because hell, you know it was Christmas and the whole student body couldn't be totally pissed and cynical.

But that third year, Matt had been drinking and horsing around the day before the concert, when classes were sort of over. There was a lot of snow on the ground, and he and some of the other guys had this idea that it would be fun to make a bonfire in the woods, just a little ways from their dorm but still out of sight. And so that night, hours after they had snuck out and were good and drunk, they started this bonfire, and it lit up the clearing, and the snow reflected the jumping flames up onto the red faces of the boys as they whooped with glee at their fire, and started singing "Hallelujah Amen" as a drinking song, and danced around the fire, hopping around in that weird half-light of the eastern winter as the wind picked up and blew a bunch of the sparks through the air, and the sparks landed on two of the boys and their jackets caught fire.

One of the boys was Matt McCulloch. His sleeve caught fire, and he saw the same happen to the other boy, but he just shoved his arm in the snow and watched the other boy run into the woods. Matt McCulloch had always been scared of the woods.

The other boy was drunk and took a second to realize he was on fire, and in the chorus of *amen amen hallelujah amen* he was sort of lost, and when he ran off into the woods no one really noticed but Matt, and as the boys all hit the fun loud part of *king of kings, forever, and ever, and lord of lords,* that kid's jacket melted onto his skin and he passed out from shock; and in the woods, about forty feet from Matt and the other boys, the flames devoured all his clothing and much of his skin, and his corpse lay naked but for the melted vestiges of his parka, in the fresh, clean, cold snow of the New England forest.

And so Matt McCulloch remembers being in trouble as a teenager, even though he was never in any real trouble. No one found out that Matt had known the kid never came in that night. Matt McCulloch vomited the next morning when the kid was discovered, but everyone attributed it to a big heart. None of the boys involved were kicked out of school, there were too many. But someone had to take the blame, there had to be action, because this was a distinguished old institution, so one of the deans was fired, and he moved to Colorado and taught at a public school, and the kids in his English classes there had an awful lot more homework than usual. Matt McCulloch and the others felt guilty for a relatively long time, or at least until they left the school and went on their way, sometimes haunted by all of this and sometimes not.

# 70

EVERYBODY TOOK ETHICS *in the eleventh grade. It was a require-*
*ment. Why, White Mike wondered. White Mike was always*
*bored in his ethics class, but he faked it and was sailing through*
*with an A until the day's topic was organized religion: discrimi-*
*nation, belief, freedom, all that. White Mike slumped back in*
*his chair and listened as his peers tried to articulate their thoughts*
*about how they liked the moral values of Christianity but still*
*thought religion was the* opium *of the masses. The black girl in*
*the class, on scholarship, started talking about how she went to*
*church every Sunday and sang, and how there was a sense of*
*community. White Mike was in a bad mood. He raised his hand,*
*and everyone looked at him, because whenever he talked, it was*
*something different.*

*"The problem is that religion is just a cop-out. So is com-*
*munity. It's just out of loneliness, you know, something to hold*
*on to when you can't do it yourself. It's for weak people. Strength*
*in adhering to values? No, it's not." The black girl looked close to*
*tears. The teacher was trying to interrupt, but White Mike wasn't*

*stopping. He looked the teacher right in the eye.* Look what I'm about to do.

"*Because really, when you get down on your knees on the pew, you're just giving God a blow job.*"

"*Get out, Mike,*" said the teacher, pointing to the door. "*Just get out.*"

# 71

WHITE MIKE KNOWS there will be no skateboarders at night in the winter, but when he calls this kid Andrew back, he tells him to meet at the amphitheater in the park where the skaters go. White Mike gets there early and stands on the stage and looks around at the benches and the snow, still unbroken in places, reflecting blue and white from the light of streetlamps.

White Mike sees the kid coming from a long way off, looking all around, over his shoulder and everything. White Mike rolls his eyes at the kid's approach. *Why did I tell the kid to meet me here,* wonders White Mike. *It's like the damn movies. Except it's a fifty. Right.*

Andrew thinks, *Damn, this is a drug deal* when he sees the tall pale guy in the dark overcoat standing in the shadows of the theater.

"Hello." Andrew can't think of anything else to say.

"Hi." White Mike has never had a kid say hello before.

"Umm, well, here you go." Andrew hands over the money.

White Mike looks in the kid's eyes. "You're not going to do this ever again, are you?"

"I hope not. No offense or anything."

"You might not even be the one smoking this, right?"

"No, probably." Andrew hadn't expected the dealer to be so talkative.

"But since you're not about to be a regular, you want to tell me something?"

"Should we be just standing around here like this?"

"It's fine. But we can walk. I know you want to go. But you can walk with me out of the park. Andrew, right?"

"I guess." They start walking.

"Why the weed?"

"A girl I know wanted it, so I'm sort of picking it up for her."

"She shouldn't smoke it if she's not brave enough to buy it."

"I don't know."

"If that's enough for you, then good, I guess."

"What?"

"Well, your life is about girls."

"No, it's not."

"You're out buying weed for one."

"Yeah, but there's more."

"What?"

"Well, everything. New Year's Eve tomorrow."

"So?"

"I don't know what the fuck you're talking about—" Andrew stops short and reminds himself, *You're talking to a drug dealer.*

White Mike shoves his hands in his pockets and doesn't say anything.

A light snow begins falling as they turn out of the park at Seventy-second Street. The flakes are very white in the air, falling through the light of the lamps, and the soft sound that comes with snow descends.

"Good luck with the girl."

"Yeah. Thanks for the weed."

"Anytime."

"Good luck to you too, I guess, in dealing or whatever. I hope it works out."

White Mike turns downtown, and Andrew watches the snowflakes pile on the shoulders of his overcoat as he walks away.

*That must be the wackest drug dealer ever,* thinks Andrew.

# 72

WHITE MIKE WENT to *Times Square the previous New Year's Eve. It was what he expected, a huge drunken confluence of humanity, hookers and crooks and fools from the bridges and tunnels and, of course, teenage drug dealers. White Mike arrived in Midtown on the late side, so he couldn't get anywhere near Times Square itself. The mass of bodies extended blocks and blocks in every direction. White Mike wondered if Dick Clark somehow soaked up all this energy from doing it year after year and that was what made him look maybe forty years younger than he actually was. Anyway, there was an energy. White Mike liked it. He liked moving through the crowds alone, sneaking through the police barricades and watching everything flow by around him.*

*The crowd extended up to Central Park South, and White Mike climbed a tree on the park side and sat in it looking down Seventh Avenue and could just make out Times Square. It wasn't snowing, but the cold was blistering, and White Mike wished for a second that he smoked, because he bet it would have made him warmer.*

*When the ball dropped, the crowd below went wild and White Mike watched everybody make out. It was cold, but White Mike liked it in the tree, so he stayed there for a long time and watched the crowd disperse in all the different directions. When he came down and started walking home, the city was still wired, and there were crowds of people in the park, and in front of the dome where the skaters came, there were a lot of people dancing. On the stage was some terrible salsa band with a thumping techno beat and lights flashing on the dancers. The crowd was young and old, everybody drunk and dancing in the freezing cold. White Mike was almost tempted to dance but didn't and kept walking. When he got over to Fifth Avenue, he decided against going home and headed back downtown. It was very bright, and there were still crowds moving across the city like small storms.*

*Outside an expensive restaurant, White Mike saw a lady with a lined face and knit gloves biting her thumb and crying. She looked terrified and reminded White Mike of the refugees he had seen on CNN. Her hair was pulled back, but wisps of it were flying loose, and her scrunched-up face was so terrible and haunting that White Mike looked at her twice. He realized that she was whimpering and biting her way through the glove, and he thought that her thumb must be getting all mangled. Next to her, two couples in evening clothes were walking into the restaurant.*

*White Mike turned back into the crowds of people. He wanted to be far away. Just way the fuck gone from this whole city. This place where people chewed off their own hands while the people next to them sipped champagne in tuxedos.*

Get hold of yourself, *he thought.* Don't be an asshole.

# 73

ON THE WAY home from selling to Andrew, White Mike is thinking about loneliness. He is feeling the change in his pocket. The streets are almost empty, but there is always someone out. Because there are millions of people here.

*How many is a million,* thinks White Mike. *What are there millions of? People. Pigeons. Pennies. Everybody knows what a penny dropped from the top of the Empire State Building can do. So if it started to rain pennies, millions of pennies, and these tiny bronze disks were streaking to the earth, catching the sunlight, the bronze rain would explode into the pavement and leave craters and you would run for cover. And there you would be, hiding under some overhang with everyone else who has run for cover, pressed in against the other bodies taking shelter. If it started raining money.*

*White Mike didn't spend much time down at the restaurants with his dad anymore. It just wasn't worth it to go there and pretend to work, because the work his father put him to was so easy that White Mike finished it in no time. And what was the point? To learn the business? His dad never noticed when he left, just so long as White Mike had dinner with him every once in a while, usually in an Italian restaurant a few blocks from home. And White Mike never asked for spending money, so that wasn't a problem. And the restaurants were always there, so he was busy that way if he needed to be.*

*A month ago, White Mike's father told him that instead of going to work, they should do something else, spend some time together. Doing what, his father didn't say. White Mike got up at ten and his father got up at twelve, and by the time his father was ready to go out, it was one. They didn't talk much at lunch, except for his father running down some problems with one of the restaurants. They got back home around three-thirty, and then the phone rang and White Mike's father took the call in his room.*

*White Mike heard the sibilant S's through the door as his father spoke on the phone with his girlfriend. It was quiet, but the hissing sound carried through the apartment. White Mike knew his father wouldn't come out of his room, so he sat with his back against the opposite wall and his feet touching the closed door. He sat and listened to his father but not the words, just the sound through the door, like gas escaping some fractured mechanism. White Mike wondered what his father had to talk about for so long, because as he sat there, the sun, which was casting short white squares of light from the windows, dropped low, and the light lengthened and faded, and White Mike watched it creep to his leg and spill over onto his knees and pass him completely and continue up the floor. And it was just so fucking lonely, the light lengthening and darkening. When he heard the click of the re-*

ceiver, White Mike got up quickly and went to his room, where he kept checking his beeper, hoping for a call.

White Mike's father apologized later for the phone call, but he knew his son would understand, and you know, Mike, how it is with women.

# 74

ON THE TWENTIETH floor at Eighty-first and Third Avenue, Molly leans her head out the window way up there in the sky and looks toward the park, halfway across town. She has taken out her contact lenses, so the sharp headlights of the cars are out of focus and the street appears to her a great river of lights, shimmering circles of yellow and red, obscuring the shapes of the cars and the edges of the building and all the people. The circles speed past beneath her, and the sounds of the street and the horns rise from them, but way up there in the sky, without her glasses on or her contacts in, the movement of the lights is so smooth that the sharp sounds seem disjointed, not to fit with anything.

Molly wears clothing very well, though she never picks it out in advance. But tonight she is trying on different outfits for the next night, and ten minutes after she has begun, she looks in the mirror and sees herself trying on a short black skirt and a tank top and jutting her hips out to the side. She double-takes in the mirror, furrows her eyebrows, and yells at the reflection,

"I am not a tank-top girl! I am not, I am not," and she rips off all her clothing and tosses the tank top out the window and stands there naked and cold. She sticks her head out the window to see where the garment has landed. It is in the trees, twenty stories down. Molly gets into bed and sleeps naked.

# Part V
# New Year's Eve

# 75

WHITE MIKE DIDN'T do drugs, but Hunter did once in a while. *The most important time was one night last December. Hunter told White Mike what he was going to do, and White Mike said he was a fool, but Hunter was determined, so White Mike was of course going to watch out for him. They started at Ninety-sixth Street on Park, looking all the way down to the MetLife Building at the bottom, beyond all the lights on the trees. They started late so the street would be deserted. It was a Sunday night, with a full moon, and it was really very bright outside, with the lights and the moon and everything. And then Hunter started tripping out, which was the plan, and White Mike started walking him down the divider in the middle of Park Avenue, weaving him among the lighted trees and stopping him whenever cars raced by.*

*Every time a car passed by, it seemed to Hunter that the noise was as loud as thunder. The sky was so clear there couldn't be a storm coming, but the thunder he heard was so loud. And then he saw clouds, thick and black, start rolling across the sky, and covering up the stars, but the moon was so bright that when it was* covered, it was like the moon had blasted out a hole in the clouds. And then, only for Hunter, a light drizzle started to fall.

White Mike was watching his friend. Hunter kept looking up like he was afraid, as if something were coming out of the sky, but not rain. So White Mike looked up too, and he saw the stars. He recalled some melodramatic kid in his class, maybe actually Hunter, who had written in an English assignment that the stars never shine over New York, or that it was so bright you couldn't see them. But White Mike could see them now, so he thought what a crock that was. You can always see the stars if you want. It's just that no one is out late enough to get a good look at them. And a big van rolled by fast.

And Hunter felt the crack of thunder in his bones, and with it, the sky split and the rain really started coming down, and he could see White Mike walking next to him, and it was like all the moonlight was shining on him and keeping him dry, because now it was raining so hard that the streets were starting to flood, though White Mike was still dry. Hunter felt the water start rising to his knees. And as they passed the next tree wrapped in lights, it burst into flame, and as the water rose to quench the flames, the smoke was unbearable, and Hunter frantically waved his hands in front of his face to clear the smoke.

White Mike watched Hunter waving his hands and grabbed his shoulder to stop him from walking into the street before the light turned. Down on the MetLife Building there was a huge cross of lights. White Mike hadn't noticed the cross before, and he thought it was weird not to notice until now.

When Hunter emerged from the smoke, he had to push through the water because it was up to his hips, and the cross down the avenue jumped out at him from behind the burning trees, and *the MetLife sign above it expanded, and Hunter realized,* Oh, it must stand for Metropolitan Life, here is Metropolitan Life, *and the letters appeared over the building, over the cross. And something didn't seem right. The water was flooding higher and higher. Hunter thought if he could just get to the cross, he could walk on the water, hahaha, like Jesus. And he looked at White Mike and thought,* Okay, *and the two of them rose up and started walking on the water. But then Hunter looked behind him, and he saw that Park Avenue was buried in a slate-green ocean, and the sky above was sending down forks of lightning, and the water was rolling back and forth and threatening to knock down the buildings. And there was smoke rising from the water where the burning trees had been extinguished.*

*White Mike was worried now. He hoped Hunter wasn't having a bad trip, whatever, exactly, that was. But his friend kept looking over his shoulder like something terrible was coming after him.*

*Hunter saw what was happening. He and White Mike were sinking, because all the water was rolling back toward Ninety-sixth Street, collecting there at the top of the hill. And Hunter was on the ground walking again, and he was below the cross at the MetLife Building. And as he looked, he saw a wave rise up and fly toward him, towering even above the buildings, rising out of the canyon. And the wave was so dark it was black, and it blocked out the moon, and it was bearing down on him and White Mike. And the image was suddenly there in his mind, forever, of this wave crashing down Park Avenue, and the trees on fire hundreds of feet below the crest, and the flames reflected off the inside of the face, and the water then looked dull orange and green, and the moon suddenly shot through with its white light.*

*White Mike could tell that Hunter was doing badly. He turned him around so they were facing uptown, and he looked to hail a cab. They stood waiting.*

*Hunter stood there as the wave came close and grew taller and the sound was a roar, louder than the thunder, and it filled his ears and he started yelling to try and drown it out as a cab pulled up next to them.*

*"Easy, Hunter," White Mike was saying, because Hunter had started yelling in the cab, and the cabbie had gotten nervous and was making as if to pull over. White Mike threw a twenty through the partition and told the guy to keep driving.*

# 76

ANDREW WAKES UP nervous. He fell asleep in his clothes on top of his bed, and he is sticky and uncomfortable and nervous. Today is the day of the party, and he doesn't go to parties like this. They happen, but he never goes, never hears about them till afterward. So when he showers, he wonders if he should have waited till later in the day because that might make his skin look better and he wants to look good when he goes to the party tonight, when he sees Sara. Maybe he should take two showers. He masturbates in the shower because he doesn't want to seem too horny if he ends up hooking up with her, which he understands is a long shot. Maybe he'll masturbate again if he takes another shower. Sara has a boyfriend, for chrissakes. He ignores this. There will probably be other girls at the party. He puts on jeans and a sweatshirt and makes himself eggs, scrambled with cheese and tomato and pastrami, then pours a glass of orange juice. He eats fast and does the dishes. He is nervous, and surprised that he is nervous, butterflies in the stomach even, this early in the day. What to do today, he thinks.

Today is really about tonight. Maybe he'll get a haircut. That's it. A haircut. You always look good after a haircut, if it is a good haircut.

At the Unisex Hair Connection, Andrew looks through the window at a forty-year-old homosexual with blond hair in a ponytail, tight black jeans, and shirt open down to his chest. The homosexual is cutting a woman's hair. Andrew decides he wants an old-fashioned barbershop. He wonders, idly, if he is homophobic. He doesn't have any gay friends. He knows hardly any gay people. There is only one openly gay kid at school, and Andrew doesn't know him. But he knows he'd rather go to an old-fashioned barbershop. He thinks he remembers where one is, way over on Eighty-first Street.

There is a red and white barber's pole and a faded red awning that reads THREE STAR BARBER SHOP. Andrew walks in.

There are only three chairs in the place, in a row facing the big mirror. All of them are occupied. The three barbers are all short, all old, and all bald. They also strike Andrew as of the same demeanor and level of skill. They energetically, though carefully, snip away at their patrons, all of whom are middle-aged white guys in suits. It is lunchtime, and they have come to get old-fashioned haircuts.

Andrew moves his hands over the magazine rack next to the chair he waits in. There are many magazines; *Esquire* and *Entertainment Weekly* and *Sports Illustrated,* but Andrew is drawn to the bright colors and lurid nipple detail of *Playboy* and *Hustler.* Shocked, he hastily covers them up and moves down the rack to pick up the day's papers. His eyes just move over the paper as he considers how they could have magazines like those in the waiting area. Weren't they just jerk-off books? What would you do with them here? Read them while you waited for the old short bald dudes to cut your hair? Talk about the women in them with other waiting customers, like *Take a look at those!*

All three barbers finish at the same time and look at him. Via the mirror, Andrew watches himself approach one of the chairs. The little man asks him, in a thick South American accent, what he wants. Andrew makes vague motions around his ears and says, "Just a trim, you know, clean it up a little bit, not too short." The man nods and goes to work snipping around the ears. Andrew stares into the mirror, watching every cut. He worries that he should have been more specific but says nothing. When the barber moves to the back of his neck, he is confronted with all the short fuzz that runs haphazardly down Andrew's nape. The barber leaves for a moment, and Andrew anticipates the pleasant buzz of the electric trimmer. When the barber returns, though, he puts hot shaving cream on the back of Andrew's neck. Andrew sits up straight.

He still does not really have to shave; every once in a while, maybe once a week, he takes a safety razor to his face, dodging pimples and forgoing any shaving cream. And now, for the first time, there is shaving cream on his body, and the barber has a straight razor that he is stropping on a piece of leather. Andrew has never seen a straight razor outside of the movies; it is thinner and keener than he expected, not the horror-movie death instrument, although it does catch the light. Andrew feels its sharp edge run against the back of his neck. Even, long pulls as the barber moves up and down and flicks the spent shaving cream into the sink every couple of strokes. When he is finished, he wipes Andrew's neck and asks if Andrew would like a full shave. Andrew almost asks "of what," but considers it a milestone to be asked. He declines.

The haircut costs thirteen dollars, and Andrew notes the ten-dollar difference between that and what it would have cost at the Unisex Hair Connection. He walks out with the clean feeling of a new haircut and runs his hand through his hair a bunch of times. He stops and views his reflection in windows. How does the haircut look? He is not sure. On the way home, he gets a sandwich for lunch. The day is winding down. It is time to really start getting ready.

Naked in front of a mirror at home, he gives himself a full going-over, like a panning shot in a movie, the kind that starts at the toes and works its way to the head, except that it usually happens for women. Andrew looks at toes, shins, knees, thighs, balls, cock, pubic hair, faint traces of "treasure trail" between pubic hair and navel, navel, stomach, ribs, nipples, clavicle, neck, and finally face. Special attention is given to the new haircut.

Andrew decides he looks bad. He is doomed. It is too short. It makes his forehead look too big and accentuates his pimples. He is all red, like the rotten mangoes his mother recently threw away. Who eats mangoes in the winter in New York, anyway? *Not me,* thinks Andrew. *So they went bad and got thrown away.*

Andrew puts on a clean shirt, Quicksilver, dark blue and stylish, and spends the next fours hour in front of his TV waiting until it's time to go to the party. He plans to get there at ten; he wants to be sure that Sara will already be there because, he realizes unhappily, he won't know anybody. Or he probably will. Everybody knows everybody. Sara said to come early, because kids would be there early and then all night.

Andrew decides that tonight might be one of those rare occasions on which he will get himself drunk.

## 77

MOLLY WAKES UP and jumps rope. It is her favorite exercise. She was queen of double Dutch at school. It was funny. There had been a kid in her class from the program that brought poor kids to the private schools. The girl introduced all her new white friends to double Dutch when they were in the first grade, and during recess that was what the girls would do. Molly was great at it. Years later, when nobody jumped rope in recess anymore, Molly still wanted to, so she bought one and jumped at home. She thought that when she exercised, she felt better. She did it sometimes when she was nervous too.

So now she is in her room gracefully jumping rope. The ceiling above her has black marks in one place where the rope slaps the ceiling every second with the same sound. Molly is counting down from one hundred; ninety-nine, ninety-eight, ninety-seven, all the way down to zero. *All it is,* thinks Molly, as she feels a burning in her calves, *is the endurance of time.*

*I know I'm going to work and do the hard thing and be good. There's no equivocation, so it's really just waiting it out. I know I'm going to keep jumping, so it's just getting past sixty, fifty-nine, fifty-eight, fifty-seven . . .*

# 78

CHRIS DECIDES WHEN he wakes up that he had better go buy some condoms, in case he finally gets laid tonight. Pops his cherry. Fucks her brains out. Fucks her raw. Fucks her hard. Fucks her from behind. Fucks her gratuitously. Taps that ass. Gets with her. Gets some. Gets in. Gets it on. Pokes her. Bangs her. Boinks her. Scores.

Does the hibbity-dibbity.

But what monster is more heinous than the man behind the counter. Chris walks casually into the drugstore. It is large, with the condoms in the back behind the pharmacy check-out. He grabs a plastic basket and prowls the rows of deodorants, picking one out. He gets some shampoo and a razor. He picks up some hydrogen peroxide, tosses it in his basket. Then, with an air of finality, he strolls to the back of the store and the condom display behind the counter. He makes as if to pay, then gives an audible *oh* and snaps his fingers: "Could I also have a pack of Trojans, please?"

"Which ones?" The man motions up and down the dizzy-ing wall of contraceptives.

"Oh, umm," *think fast, think fast,* "regular's fine." *Please God, let there be a regular.*

The man hands him a pack of condoms. Chris pays for everything and leaves, walking as fast as he casually can.

# 79

BACK HOME, the maids are cleaning up. They'll be gone by five. Chris suspects people will start showing up not long after that. It's not like they have anywhere else to go.

Chris doesn't have much to do in the way of party preparation. He doesn't bother to move any of the valuable stuff, but he does rearrange his room beyond what the maid usually does. He has stuff that he doesn't want seen. He checks his stash of pornography and decides that it is well enough hidden (behind a grate in the ceiling). Then he thinks, *I'm about to get laid. I'll never need porn again. From now on I can get someone else to whack it.*

So he takes all his porn, a great armful, and shoves it into a garbage bag. He carries the bag downstairs, knowing that the garbage gets taken out every two days, and dumps it in the can behind the kitchen. Chris is elated by this disposal, feels liberated as he climbs the stairs to play video games for a couple of hours before showering and taking great care dressing himself.

# 80

WHITE MIKE GOT a pair of high-powered binoculars from his father for Christmas one year, and he looked into different windows with them. He never saw anything that interesting, but there was one window across the street that he had a good view into and liked a lot. It was a living room, and a family of five watched television and ate dinner in the room. White Mike imagined the times and travails of the family, and though he could not make out their features that clearly, he invented personas for all of them. There were two boys and a girl and the parents. The entire family, White Mike saw, was redheaded. The kids watched The Simpsons almost every night. The parents occasionally fought, and once White Mike saw them making out on the couch. He made a point of checking on them regularly. It was another one of the things he did. Like, it's eight-thirty, time to check on the Joyces, which is what he named them.

White Mike did not feel guilty about watching them. He didn't stay to watch the parents kiss on the couch because that felt

*weird, but otherwise, he watched. White Mike didn't know why.*
*Maybe, he thought, it was just voyeurism. Or maybe he was liv-*
*ing through them. Whatever. Families interested him.*

What the fuck, Mike, *he thought.* What do you do? You
watch a family through a window with binoculars every night
at eight-thirty. Fucking loser.

# 81

ON THE WAY back to his room from the shower, Chris pauses at his brother's door and knocks. There is no answer, but he can hear his brother padding around the room. Chris knocks again, harder. He hears the padding feet come closer to the door, and it opens a crack. It looks dark inside.

"Claude, you know I'm having an open house tonight. You know, like you used to have."

"Yeah."

"So I just wanted you to know, there'll be a bunch of kids here. Maybe some pussy for you."

"Whatever." Claude thinks about how he might engrave the handle of his sword.

"Tobias is coming. He's bringing some model from one of his shoots."

"Whatever."

"What're you doing in there, Claude?" Chris is thinking about how into these kind of parties Claude used to be.

"Nothing. Later." Claude closes the door in his brother's face, turns around, and sees his room in candlelight. He has drawn all the curtains and blacked out all light from the outside. Every candle in the house has been gathered and is now alight and flickering before him. More chips have been hewn from the wall. In front of the full-length mirror on the door to Claude's bathroom, there is a circle of candles on the floor. Another half circle surrounds the weapons closet. Locking the door, Claude goes back to the closet, opens it, and admires how the candlelight shines along the steel of his weapons. He takes out the sword, razor-sharp from his furious sharpening that morning, and walks over to the circle before the mirror. He stands in it and takes off his shirt. He is wearing jeans only, and he looks at himself in the mirror in the circle of candles, the sword in his hand. He looks quite attractive, like some sort of action hero at the climax of the movie. Just what he wants to look like. Claude is glad he stopped taking drugs. This is better.

# 82

AS ALWAYS, White Mike notices the tops of the buildings as he walks. He sees gargoyles and urns in relief, and various edifices repeating in similar patterns from building to building, a function of zoning laws that requires new buildings in the best neighborhoods to be constructed to match the style of the neighboring buildings. They don't actually have to have solid cornices, as long as they look the same. The projecting cornices and gargoyles on some of the new buildings are in fact not stone but rather hollow, weather-resistant plaster. So White Mike knows that if he has to jump from rooftop to rooftop, he will have to be careful not to catch himself on any of the projecting cornices or gargoyles as he is landing, for while some of them would hold, others would snap and crumble.

White Mike knows he will never jump from rooftop to rooftop, even though he wishes he could. Just like he knows he's never going to fly. That is what he is thinking as he hails a cab to go to the special bird bookstore he has discovered in Midtown.

*   *   *

In the last year White Mike has gotten interested in birds and has read a lot of books about them, especially parrots. He has ordered some of them off of Amazon.com but gets most from the bookstore he is going to now. He has a decent little ornithological library. White Mike likes the whole idea of flight, and if anybody ever asked him, he could explain in scientific detail the mechanisms of the wing. He likes owls and condors and ospreys, but nothing has ever captured him quite like the parrot. Pirates had parrots. White Mike even considered getting a parrot and teaching it to talk, although he doesn't know what he would have it say.

Of course, he knows parrots don't think. They just imitate, just repeat. *But that's okay,* thinks White Mike. *Everybody sort of does that. And my bird will say the smartest shit you ever heard. None of this teaching the bird to curse or any of that.* The humor behind teaching parrots to say *fuck you* baffles him.

Such humor does not baffle Timmy or Mark Rothko. When the two of them, sitting on a stoop in the Fifties, see none other than White Mike get out of a cab and get buzzed into a nondescript building there on Madison Avenue, they are intrigued. First, because they smoked all their weed and need some more. And second, because they have nothing to do, and yo it's White Mike.

Mark Rothko flicks his cigarette into the street like a tiny, angry miner. He follows Timmy toward the building, where they wait for a half hour until White Mike comes out.

"Yo, Miiike!"

White Mike just looks at them.

"Whas in there?" Timmy points at the small bundle of books White Mike is holding protectively.

"Some weed?" Mark Rothko asks hopefully.

"Books," says White Mike.

"Yo, sorry, Mike. We gotta get some mo of dat shit."

"Beep me later." White Mike starts walking toward home. Timmy and Mark Rothko follow.

"What are you doing?" White Mike says.

"We comin' with you, man."

"No you're not."

"Yes we are, we gonna score some Chronic, yeah baby, yeah," says Timmy. Mark Rothko nods in agreement and takes out another cigarette. White Mike looks down at the two of them and almost laughs. But he doesn't want these kids following him home, so he tells them that he'll work out a special deal for them if they get lost now and beep him later.

"Yo, we got the hookup." Timmy practically jumps for happiness but is held down by his girth, low center of gravity, and cargo pants.

"Foh shizza my drizzle," Mark Rothko concurs.

"What? Actually, never mind. You won't follow me now, right? Otherwise, no weed."

"Yeah, fo' sho."

White Mike leaves them behind, but he has overestimated the power of his deal, because Timmy and Mark Rothko wait until he is two blocks ahead and then follow. They think maybe they'll find out where White Mike lives.

A block from home, White Mike gets something else he wants—a milk shake from Häagen-Dazs. They cost five dollars each. They are the best milk shakes in the city, in the world, as far as he knows. He chews on the straw and drinks it on his way home, so that the longer he has it, the more difficult it becomes to suck the sugary stew up out of the cup.

Mark Rothko and Timmy watch fascinated as their drug dealer drinks his milk shake. Mark Rothko thinks: *I'm gonna get one of those later.* He and Timmy follow White Mike down the last block to his apartment building. They stand across the street after he lets himself in. It is a small prewar building that looks just like hundreds of other buildings in the city, but not to Timmy and Mark Rothko—it is where White Mike lives.

White Mike is sitting at the kitchen table, sipping the last of his milk shake and looking at his new books, when Timmy and Mark Rothko buzz up.

"Hello?"

"Yo, it us."

White Mike is pissed and goes downstairs quick to run them off.

"You little fuckers aren't getting any more weed, ever."

"Awwww, man . . ." Timmy realizes their big mistake.

"Goddammit, Timmy. Now we'll never get blizzy." Mark Rothko is pissed too.

"Get out of here."

The two don't move for a second, and White Mike looks from one to the other. Just a couple of soft kids standing on the street, trying to get some weed, have some fun, fill the time, talk a certain way, dress a certain way, walk a certain way, be a certain way because the way they come from is unclear and uncool and with no direction, because no one really has anything to do, all across the city no one has anything to do, so they all do the same thing and make the same references to pop culture and their childhood cartoons (like, *Ghostbusters* was so much better than *Ninja Turtles*), and everyone wants to get laid and be the cool kid and everyone wants to be a jock, and everyone wants and wants and wants. White Mike is worried now about what will happen if other kids start showing up at his door. And White Mike doesn't want to give anybody else weed. So White Mike lets the two kids in.

After he gives Timmy and Mark Rothko their weed, he tells them he is going to get a bird, a parrot.

"That talks?" asks Timmy.

"Yeah," says White Mike. "What should I name him?"

"Timmy," suggests Timmy.

"Rocko," suggests Mark Rothko.

"Rocko?"

"Yeah. So?"

"Nothin'."

"Tupac."

"Biggie."

"Sylvester."

"It's a guy bird, right?"

"Yeah."

"How do you know? Do they have dicks?"

"I dunno."

"Fine. Samantha."

"Samantha?"

"'S my mother's name, son."

"Yo, sorry."

"How 'bout Snoop?"

White Mike thinks immediately of Charlie Brown. "That's not a bad name," he says.

Timmy and Mark Rothko burst into song:

"D-o-double-juh-zeee."

"Snooop Daawwg."

"Smoke till yo' eyes get cataracts."

"Snooop Daawwg."

"Who's that dippin' in the Cadillac?"

"Snooop Daawwg."

"All right, enough." White Mike shuts them up. "Snoop it is. Snoop the parrot." Timmy and Mark Rothko nod triumphantly at each other.

"We call you tomorrow when we got the kiggity cash flow?"

"Fine."

When they are gone, White Mike sits for a long time, thinking about adults. He is trying to pinpoint the exact moment when he didn't want to talk to them anymore. The only adults he talks to now are the ones he doesn't care so much about but has some kind of business with. Like Lionel. His beeper vibrates, and he takes it out of his pocket and puts it on the table, where it rattles violently. White Mike turns it on and off quickly to stop the shaking, at least for now.

# 83

HUNTER IS ON the phone with his father, who is in a limo coming in from JFK. Hunter's voice is cracking for the first time since he was arrested.

"I didn't kill anyone. I mean, who kills people. Don't you get this, Dad? Dad?"

"Hunter, I'm here now, we'll take care of things, talk to the judge about bail—"

"No one kills people. Not me. I mean, come on."

"Hunter, you have to calm down."

"Dad, I'll tell you straight out that I'm innocent, but I am scared as shit, Dad, but I know that if it was you in here, you'd be more scared."

Hunter's father doesn't say anything.

# 84

AFTER THEY LEAVE White Mike's apartment, Timmy and Mark Rothko go to the grocery store.

On the way, Timmy asks: "What did the parrot say to the nigga?"

"What?"

"'Polly wanna cracka.'"

Mark Rothko laughs.

"And waz the nigga say to the parrot?"

"What?" Guffaws.

"'Fuck you, bitch,' and then he busts a cap in the parrot's ass."

They're both cracking up.

"We need munchies. C'mon." Timmy walks through the automatic doors of the grocery store. He heads to the crackers and picks up a box of saltines. He has lost Mark Rothko momentarily, but in the next aisle he finds him with his hand in a jar of Marshmallow Fluff, a portion of the sticky white substance already smeared on his collar and chin. A lady with a shopping cart moves away quickly. Timmy says: "Word, word, lemme get summa that."

Timmy opens up a column of saltines and starts dipping them in the fluff. The two of them keep working on the Fluff until they see a supermarket worker arrive at the open end of the aisle to stack jams. Timmy stashes the rest of the crackers in his pocket, and Mark Rothko drops the jar of Fluff, which breaks on the floor. Timmy and Mark Rothko beat a sticky retreat back to the automatic doors. They got a party to go to. The supermarket worker has a hell of a time cleaning the viscous confection off the floor.

# 85

THE PHONE RINGS. It is late afternoon, and White Mike is eating Cheerios. He used to go in for all the sugary-type cereals
but recently switched to simple Cheerios, so the Cocoa Puffs
are rotting into plastic fungus in the cupboard. Mike uses a tea-
spoon to eat his cereal, not a big soup spoon, because he likes
less milk in his mouth with each bite. The phone keeps ringing. White Mike picks it up. It is his father telling him not to
go anywhere, that he is coming home and has something to tell
him. He is holding his voice steady and level.

"What?" asks White Mike. "What is it?"

"I'll tell you when I get there."

"Tell me now. I'd rather know now."

"Let me tell you when I get there."

"I can take it. Just tell me. Better I know now."

"I'm serious, Mike."

White Mike is caught off guard by the inflection in his
father's voice. They are both silent for a moment. When White

Mike hears his father's voice on the other end of the line again, it is hard and flat.

"Charlie is dead. He was murdered three days ago in Harlem, but they couldn't identify him. The police just called." He hangs up the phone before White Mike can say anything.

White Mike screams. An explosion out of his chest, a snarl from the bottom of his spine out into the air to make everything stop for a second while he runs and jumps into the air, off a building maybe, to tire himself out and do something about Charlie being dead and the house being a mess. So White Mike starts cleaning. First he jumps and lands on the couch on his back and flexes his whole body, knocking the pillows off, holding the scream in the very top of his chest. He thrashes until he is worn out, and then he rises and starts cleaning the house. The house is a mess: the dishes aren't done and the blinds are half drawn and there is no fresh air but you can't open the windows because the kitchen windows were built soundproof, never to be opened. He goes to the closet and gets a broom and a bucket and a mop and rags. His steps are tight and wired off his toes as he moves from floor to sink to shelves, picking things up, putting them where they belong. As soon as he has cleared every surface in the kitchen, he fills the bucket with soapy water and uses the rags to scrub. He gets on a stool and scrubs the ceiling. Then the stool wobbles and flips, and he falls to the tile floor. On his stomach, he looks out over the plane of the floor, and this is how his father finds him when he walks in the door.

White Mike and his father look at each other.

"I'm sorry, Mike."

"I have to go out. I'll be back."

"Yeah, a walk might help. I'll walk you to the end of the block."

"Whatever," White Mike says, and his father flinches.

At the end of the block, White Mike's father is telling him that the police don't know what happened, but they think maybe Charlie was involved in a drug deal. Also, they'd like to ask some questions.

White Mike shrugs, but for the first time in his life, he wonders what his father actually knows.

# 86

WHILE SHE IS getting dressed for the party, Jessica becomes distracted by her own eyes in the mirror. She wonders whether or not Twelve makes people's eyes dilate the way weed does. Whatever. She likes her eyes, big and brown. *Strong eyes, you in the mirror. Stronger than all these kids,* she is thinking. *Strong enough to get into Wesleyan, strong enough to go to that shrink, strong enough to work this party, strong enough to get dressed. Strong enough to get whatever you want. Strong enough to get the Twelve from that drug dealer. Strong enough to do whatever it takes. Strongest.*

# 87

WHITE MIKE IS walking west, into the sun. Now he turns on to Fifth Avenue, with the snow on the trees and the shadows lengthening. His mind is blank, and his hands are cold. At the north end of Central Park, he hangs a left and walks west again. He turns uptown again on the other side of the park. Up into Harlem.

He knows where he is going, the Cathedral of St. John the Divine. One of the world's biggest gothic cathedrals. Maybe the biggest. White Mike isn't sure. It casts a shadow so long he cannot see where it ends. *Why are you going here,* he thinks to himself. *Might just as well walk through Harlem and get shot yourself, like Charlie. You wouldn't get shot walking through Harlem. Who would kill Charlie?* White Mike walks faster through the cold air to the big double doors.

The ceilings are so high in this place, and it is dim inside, and there is no service or anything happening. White Mike looks at all the candles and almost lights one but doesn't because he doesn't know how to do it, really. So he just looks at them in the warm gloom for a second as he passes. Far up ahead of him, beyond what must be a thousand old church chairs, is the altar. He can hear everything and especially his own footsteps. He keeps walking past the little vestibules on the side, in the echoes of the grand building with all its oak and metal gilded opulence. Eventually he comes to the Poet's Corner, where there are inscriptions he doesn't know, the kind of stuff he would usually stop to read but doesn't. He walks to the middle of the cathedral and sits down.

*Isn't this where you're supposed to go numb,* thinks White Mike. He grips the back of the chair in front of him until his knuckles crack and turn white. The edges of his overcoat pool on the ground around the chair, and he realizes that he is hot and uncomfortable. The cathedral is very warm. He takes off his overcoat and leans his head back over the edge of his chair and stares up into the high ceiling. Out of the corner of his eye he sees someone else, an old lady, stooped and leaning forward in a chair, head down. He suddenly thinks that his posture might be uncouth, disrespectful, in this place, and he tucks in his legs and leans forward from the edge of his chair and bows his head.

White Mike sits in that chair for a long time, with his head down. And behind him in that sea of little chairs is the old lady hunched down, and somewhere else are two tourists who get up and leave pretty soon, and there are one or two others sitting far from each other. But White Mike sits there and thinks of nothing, his hands gripping the chair in front of him, his head down, and the church dim and quiet and echoey.

And then he starts thinking of Charlie, and he thinks of how Charlie must have died. He remembers a scene in a war movie when the soldier describes how the bullet penetrates the skin and you get to watch it in slow motion go into some guts and make a clean tunnel almost, and then how that tunnel fills up with green goo, bile. And then when he finishes describing it, it all happens in reverse and the tunnel disappears and the bile is gone and the skin heals and the bullet flies backward, but of course that never happens. And White Mike can't help it when he thinks of how the next scene in the movie was about how a cow stepped on a land mine and exploded and how that was mad funny. But he gets angry at himself for thinking about that and decides that the cathedral is dumb and it is time to leave. He takes his overcoat over his arm and walks out into the street.

# 88

JESSICA GETS TO Chris's house earlier than she has ever arrived at a party. She wants to be there in case Lionel is early. Not that she thinks he will be early, why would anyone be early? So she goes over to Chris's house not long after the streetlights have completely replaced the sun. It is snowing on and off. And the party gets going.

Kids from half the private schools in the city start showing up. And boarding school kids who have to leave in two days. The party is getting more and more crowded.

Jessica is talking about Twelve with some of her friends, asking them to chip in.

A bunch of kids have started doing shots in the kitchen, and someone finally figures out the house stereo, so the music plays everywhere out of the speakers in the walls. It is loud all over the house. The CD player is on shuffle, so the Stones are playing one minute, then D'Angelo, then Weezer, then all the other bands Chris has put in, something for everyone. He doesn't want to have chosen the music for himself, lest he should have to stand by it if someone brought it up.

The heavy pot smokers have already found their way up to the terrace, and in the darkness their joints are little points of light.

By this time there are close to fifty kids in the house. Sara is very happy, smiling, greeting everyone. She tells Chris to leave the front door unlocked. It is hard to hear the bell anyway.

Sitting in his room in a circle of candles, Claude can feel the house filling up. He doesn't know if he likes this.

"Jessica, do you have a number for some weed?" asks a girl in a tank top as Jessica looks at her watch and then at the door.

"Oh, yeah, fine. Here." She hands the girl her cell phone. "Hit seventeen."

# 89

WHITE MIKE WALKS out into the air, and it is snowing. The cathedral towers behind him. He knows that he was in there a long time, and he wants to go home now. He is suddenly very tired and wants to go to sleep.

In the cab, he wonders why he went to the church. Just more bullshit. *That is exactly what I don't need,* he thinks. *But that's what you do at times like this. You walk into a church even though you are not religious. And either it helps or it doesn't, but usually it doesn't and so what.*

The cab stops in front of his house, and he gives the man the whole twenty, a huge tip. The guy thanks him profusely, and White Mike says nothing back as he gets out. He just didn't feel like dealing with asking for change. It was on some weird cent, like he would have had to ask for $11.30 or something to get the tip right. The cab number is 4C46.

White Mike walks into his front hall and hears his father in the kitchen making dinner. He is standing over the stove, frying steaks in butter and lemon and wiping grease out of the pan with sourdough bread. It used to be something they liked, lemon steak, his father called it. He used to make it for Charlie too. Before either of them says anything, White Mike feels his beeper go off.

# 90

AT AROUND TEN, Jerry, the only white kid besides Hunter who goes to the Rec, arrives at the party. He is having a beer in front of one of the big TVs with a bunch of other kids. He is recounting the story of Hunter's fight—a couple of the kids know Hunter and about him being in jail.

"You think he might have done it?"

"No way," says Josh.

"I heard there were two dead guys."

"Why would Hunter kill anybody?"

# 91

LIONEL DRIVES UP to the party in his 1988 white Lincoln Town Car and double-parks in front of the ivy-covered town house. He grabs a backpack from the seat next to him and gets out and locks the car. He rings the doorbell before he realizes the door is slightly ajar, and he walks in.

Jessica has been watching the door from the stairs. She is quick to beckon Lionel upstairs to the deserted guest bedroom, across the hall from Claude's room. The room is dark except for the blue light filtering out of the piranha tank and bouncing off the cymbals and metal of the drum set.

"Let me see the money." Lionel's smooth voice floats out from under his hood as Jessica closes the door behind them.

"Oh yeah, fine, here." Jessica is nervous. *I don't have enough.*

Lionel counts, and as he is getting through the bills, Jessica interrupts and tells him, "Look, there's only five hundred there."

"I brought a thousand bag," Lionel says sharply.

*I don't have enough. Five hundred isn't enough. I don't have enough.* "It's enough." Jessica surprises herself with the anger in her voice. "You can—"

"No. I told you, I've only got thousands."

"I'm good for the rest of the money." She speaks levelly and coldly. Her eyes have deadened, this close to the drug.

"No." He turns to leave.

"Wait," she shouts, and stamps her foot. "I can give you something else."

Lionel looks around the room, noticing how expensive everything is. Good criminal judgment tells him he doesn't want to be taking anything out of here. It would be him getting busted, not the girl, if it ever came to that.

"I don't want anything from the house."

"I'll give you a blow job."

Lionel practically busts out laughing.

"I'm serious."

Lionel considers for a second as he looks at the girl, up her legs to her breasts where he stares, unabashed. She does not get embarrassed. He becomes slightly aroused, then thinks again.

"Five hundred dollars is an expensive blow job."

"I'll fuck you." And Jessica recognizes the voice coming out of her but feels far from it. She doesn't even look at Lionel, just keeps staring at the bag in his hand. "I'm a virgin."

Lionel agrees to give her the bag for two fucks. One fuck before he'll give her the bag, he says. And then she'll owe him one.

"No, the bag first, then we'll have sex."

Lionel knows he can get it back if he needs to, so he hands it to her.

Jessica sighs and steps back from Lionel, not thinking anything. She holds the bag tight, not quite sure what to do with it for a moment, before she puts it on a dresser.

She looks at Lionel and takes hold of the bottom of her sweater. She pulls it over her head, and in the blue light her pale breasts appear, supported by a simple white bra. Lionel stares and walks toward her.

## 92

BEAUTIFUL GIRLS AT the party. Two of them. Achingly beautiful. Smiling and drinking champagne. Who brought the champagne? They brought their own. They tell Sara this is, like, the best party ever. Sara takes a drink straight from their bottle. They admire her style. She spots Sean coming through the front door and waves.

The party's getting very loud. Andrew sits on a bar stool at the counter in the kitchen and watches Chris's eyes flick from the matches he is lighting one by one to the girl dancing over by the ovens, where the light from above the stove is falling down her shirt. All parties live, for a while, in the kitchen. When there are no more matches in the box, Chris moves on to a book of matches from a Thai restaurant two blocks uptown. He bends a match back, lighting it with one hand.

*Chris's mother kept saying, Chris, don't play with matches, this house is made of wood, it would go up like a tinderbox. And I hate the smell of that sulfur, please Chris. So Chris didn't play with matches in their gray shingle country home in South-hampton, at least not when his mother was there. But Claude was present during this exchange, and one night not long after his mother had fired his favorite nanny, Claude sat outside his mother's bedroom all night long, lighting matches, letting the sulfur smell seep into the room, until he heard his mother asking his father hysterically whether he smelled that horrible smell. It was the middle of the night, and his father said no, and then his mother sounded like she was crying. Good.*

Andrew looks at Chris for another second and goes to the refrigerator to get a beer, and as he is first lifting the bottle to his lips, with his fingers on either side of the neck of the bottle, holding it nonchalant-like, Molly walks into the kitchen with a girlfriend and sits down next to Chris. She is looking for Tobias but can't find him. Andrew thinks she is the most beautiful girl at the party, maybe the most beautiful he has ever seen. Beautiful like those girls in the movies. She actually looks like one of those girls. Sitting next to Chris.

"Hi," Molly says to Chris. "I'm Molly, remember, I was here the other day with your brother's friend Tobias?"

"Oh yeah. Molly, hi."

"Is this the kind of party where a sixteen-year-old girl can get drunk?"

Molly's girlfriend is smiling to see her friend flirt like this, and when she catches Molly's eye, she is practically laughing. Molly looks away.

"I'll get you a beer." Andrew gets up to get her one. He wishes it were the kind of thing that when he gave it to her, their hands had to touch.

Molly takes the beer and chugs almost the whole bottle as they all watch.

"Not very ladylike," says Chris.

"Nah, very ladylike," says Andrew.

"You some fine booty," says Mark Rothko, sidling up to Molly's chair, then turning back and sticking his hand out to Timmy. Timmy sniggers and takes a dollar from his pocket. "Here." He hands it to Mark Rothko, all the while looking at Molly.

# 93

WHITE MIKE IS walking fast, away from his apartment. He doesn't know why, but he had to get out of there. Too much stuff with the greasy meat and his father and Charlie. Out of habit, he checks his messages, as he always does when he goes out. He realizes his phone has been off. He tries to remember when it might have turned off. He is usually more careful to set the keyguard so this can't happen as the phone bounces around in his pocket. The lapse has left him with a lot of messages. Mostly beeps, but there is a voice mail from Warren, his old friend, now in Cancún.

"Hunter is in jail for murder, not joking, some kid from the Rec and a dealer, call me."

White Mike listens to the message four times, and then tries to call Warren but can't reach him. White Mike walks a little faster.

In front of a lot of the town houses in the neighborhood, there are wrought-iron gates. These fences are black and cool to the touch, and some are intricate, with curved metal and spikes and flowers. White Mike is walking even faster now, beyond his usual loose gait, and his overcoat, unbuttoned, blows out behind him when the wind gusts. The corner catches on one of the spikes of a low iron fence, and White Mike hears a rip and feels the slight vibration in the fabric as the lining tears up into the middle of his back. And now White Mike speeds up, and soon he is running up the street, over the snow in the darkness and pools of streetlight. The sidewalks are empty now, and if you can run and keep running, you will not be interrupted and you need not look both ways before you cross the street, because probably there is no car coming to skid into you, sending you into the air. White Mike feels all this and so he runs, and in his treaded shoes he does not slip on the snow, and when he sees the door of the town house and he hears the music coming out of it, he doesn't stop; he flings himself against the door. And then he is inside with the door slamming open behind him.

# 94

WHITE MIKE IS in, surrounded by a crush of kids. He knows the number that beeped him five times in a row. It is that girl Jessica. White Mike starts looking around the house. He does not slide easy past the kids standing and sitting, he pushes them out of the way, and they look at him funny, but even the drunk ones see something in him that looks terrible, and they know he isn't here for the party. He is moving too fast. He is not being cool.

White Mike doesn't like the music. He just doesn't like it. He has heard one too many Bob Marley songs at these parties. *What am I doing here? What do I care if this girl beeps me?* But White Mike always does what he's supposed to do. It is like he is on a mission. Some crazy fucking mission. Charlie's dead, murdered, Hunter's in jail for murder. And White Mike is on this mission. White Mike comes to the open closet with the house stereo system in it. And as "No Woman No Cry" comes on and he hears the first voices somewhere in the house singing along, he grabs a piece of the equipment and hurls it from the shelf to the floor.

"Oh shit," says a kid who sees him do this.

"What the fuck are you doing?" Chris appears and is yelling, but he steps back when he realizes who he is talking to.

"Who turned off the music, mon?" someone yells from the next room.

"Where's that girl?" White Mike shouts at Chris.

Chris is scared. Kids are packing into this hallway off the main hall in front of the stairs. They are standing behind Chris, seeing what will happen. This is going to make an unbelievable story when school starts again. People are going to be sorry they weren't here to see it. Sara pushes through the crowd and stands next to Chris.

"Umm, I think you better go," says Chris to White Mike.

## 95

WHEN EVERYONE ELSE runs out from the kitchen after Chris, Molly and Andrew both stay at the table. They are looking at each other. Molly takes another sip of her beer.

"That sounded like it's going to be expensive," says Andrew.

"I don't think it matters much. Is he a friend of yours?"

"Chris? Oh, no, Sara Ludlow told me about this. It's really her party. Is he your friend?"

"Don't know him."

"I've heard he's sort of a dick, actually."

"They always give the best parties, I've heard."

"What?"

"This actually isn't so bad. They'll all be back in a minute, though." She grins, and Andrew laughs.

"Whatev."

"Whatev?"

"Word."

"You mean, like, let's g?"

*"No go's* already short enough, you don't need to abbreviate it."

"No, I mean, you wanna g? Get some pizza?"

"Uhh, yeah, sure." *Booyah,* thinks Andrew.

And then a bunch of the kids come back into the kitchen, fast. Timmy and Mark Rothko lead the way.

"Shit! White Mike rocked him!"

"Word." Mark Rothko is nodding in excited disbelief.

"What happened?" Andrew asks a bunch of times before he gets an answer.

"That dealer White Mike punched Chris!"

"In the face?"

"Who?" asks Molly.

# 96

*THAT FELT SO good,* thinks White Mike.

And now White Mike is holding Chris against the wall. Sara is behind him, crying.

"I said where's that girl?"

"Upstairs somewhere, maybe."

White Mike releases Chris, and with his coat flying, he takes off up the stairs, two at a time. Chris nurses his bloody nose and feels his cheek swelling. He follows the crowd from behind, all of them following White Mike up and up, checking all the rooms.

Molly and Andrew come out of the kitchen and look up the stairs.

"That's the dealer, in the overcoat," Andrew says.

"Mike?" Molly recognizes his back, but White Mike does not hear her. By the time he is outside the guest bedroom, every kid in the house is looking at him, crowded on the banisters, as he slams open the door.

# 97

"WHAT THE FUCK?" Lionel says, and rolls, naked, off the far side of the bed. He pulls a small, shiny .38 Special with a bright white pearl handle from his parka on the floor and stands up, pointing it at White Mike, erection wilting fast. His regular gun is in the other pocket. Jessica is covering herself with the sheet.

White Mike recognizes Charlie's gun. "Oh man," he says.

"Fuck," says Lionel, lowering the gun. "What do you want?"

"I don't know," White Mike says, but he takes a step toward Lionel, and Lionel is startled by the look in his eyes. He raises the gun again.

"I know that gun. Charlie's gun, Lionel."

"He was on some shit, and he pulled it on me."

"And you killed him and took it."

"What the fuck." Lionel holds the pistol level.

White Mike just stares at him.

"You'd a shot him too."

And then White Mike launches himself across the room, grabbing for the gun, thinking he is going to kill Lionel.

Lionel fires two shots. One of the bullets hits White Mike, who falls heavily into the drum set. The other bullet hums just over Jessica's head and explodes the aquarium, and the water spills onto Jessica and the bed, and the piranhas are snapping their jaws and flopping in the broken tank. Lionel grabs his clothes and is out the door and into the hall, naked. All the kids start running down the stairs. Claude's door flies open, and he is suddenly huge in the hall, a sword strapped to his back, the Uzi in one hand.

Claude pulls the trigger of the Uzi, and it is louder than even he has ever imagined. He sees all these kids streaming down the stairs. Then he sees Molly, terrified, coming toward him, looking for White Mike. Claude points the gun at her and fires, and hits Molly many times. Andrew is right behind her and Claude kills him too. He keeps firing down the stairs and several other kids fall.

One of them is Timmy, and Mark Rothko, right beside him, stops to try and help, but Claude is now walking down the stairs and shoots Mark Rothko full in the face. Timmy sees Mark Rothko's head fly apart, and for a second he can think of nothing so much as a game the two of them used to play. They would throw rotten tangerines into the wall across from Mark Rothko's window, where they would explode with these satisfying splats.

Claude shoots Timmy then. And as he continues walking down the stairs, he sees his friend Tobias going out the door and Claude fires some shots at him but none of them hit, and Tobias slams the door behind him fast. The closed door stops

Lionel, who is naked still, carrying his clothes, and Claude shoots him in the back.

He kills the other kids who are lying wounded on the stairs. Three of them. They are two boys and a girl, and Claude dispatches each of them the same way, with a kind of careful candor in his gunfire that is straight and measured into the middle of their bodies. Claude saw what happened to Mark Rothko, and he doesn't like the mess that shooting someone in the head makes, because he accidentally stepped in some of Mark Rothko's brain matter as he continued down the stairs.

Claude looks back around but doesn't see his brother, who is still hiding in a corner at the top of the stairs, weeping.

The house is almost empty now. Claude walks the ground floor by himself, stopping in every room and looking at everything, taking his time. There is so much space. In the living room he looks at his mother's vases and couches and paintings on the wall, but he can't decide whether to fire his gun and destroy the room or not. It seems so neat that he is reluctant to disrupt the order. It is so quiet. He starts to leave the room in peace, but then he turns and fires, splintering the walls.

By this time the police are arriving, and their calls to him to come out float in Claude's head and he doesn't really hear them. But he knows they want him to come out, and he does, but not with his hands up. He comes out firing, and they shoot him dead before he is three steps out the front door.

# Afterword

# 98

*I couldn't have told the story any other way. I made some of it up, but most of it's true.*

*I was operated on a bunch of times and am fine.*

*It took awhile for everyone to put the pieces together. Hunter's name was cleared as soon as the ballistics were run on Lionel's gun. I kept the bullet around my neck on a string for a while, but then I took it off because I don't like jewelry. Then I kept it in a jar, and in the end I gave it to a girlfriend I had, and so she has it now.*

*I talked it over with my father and applied to college in Paris. They looked at my grades from high school, and I told them I had helped my father run one of the restaurants in the year off, so they took me. Before I left New York, I walked up to the projects and stood in the place where Charlie was shot.*

*I like Paris a lot. Last week I was walking over the Seine with some friends from school and we stopped, leaning on the edge of the bridge, and looked at Notre Dame. One of them took out a joint and passed it around. When it came to me, I was about to tell them I never smoke. But what the hell. It was okay.*

*Now, in the spring, when it starts to stay warm into the night, I walk and look around. I get to know the city better every day. I don't know why, but Paris seems a better place than New York. The vibe is different, I think, or maybe it's just that Paris is not my home.*

# Acknowledgments

I must acknowledge my superb teachers, editors, and friends Joel Doerfler, John Fogarty, Ronald Murison, Timothy Burroughs, Larry Colan, John Dore; Kit Dillon, Jeff Deutchman, Mookie Singerman, Trina Sen, Josh Singer, Steve O'Reilly, and Adella Oliver; Morgan, George and P.J.; my brother, Tom McDonell; my mother, Joanie McDonell; and finally, the real White Mike, whom I have never met, but whose excellent name I have used.